PRAISE FOR MICHAEL CISCO

"Fans of stylish and thematically sophisticated weird fiction should seek out...Cisco's visionary genius."

— *PUBLISHERS WEEKLY*

"The alchemy of words ceasing to be words, words seamlessly melting before our eyes into grandiose imagery, into soaring hallucination, into fever dreams that tap directly into our subconscious and perfectly describe emotions that cannot be described is something no author achieves with more effect than Michael Cisco."

— PAUL TREMBLAY, AUTHOR OF *THE CABIN AT THE END OF THE WORLD*

"A rivetingly strange novel in which Cisco mixes game theory, serious philosophy, SF, and dark fantasy into something at once unreal and really entrancing. Kind of like what might happen if Wyndham Lewis decided to write like M. John Harrison and had Martin Heidegger as his editor. Member is a complex, compelling work."

— BRIAN EVENSON, AUTHOR OF *LAST DAYS*

BLACK BRANE

HORROR

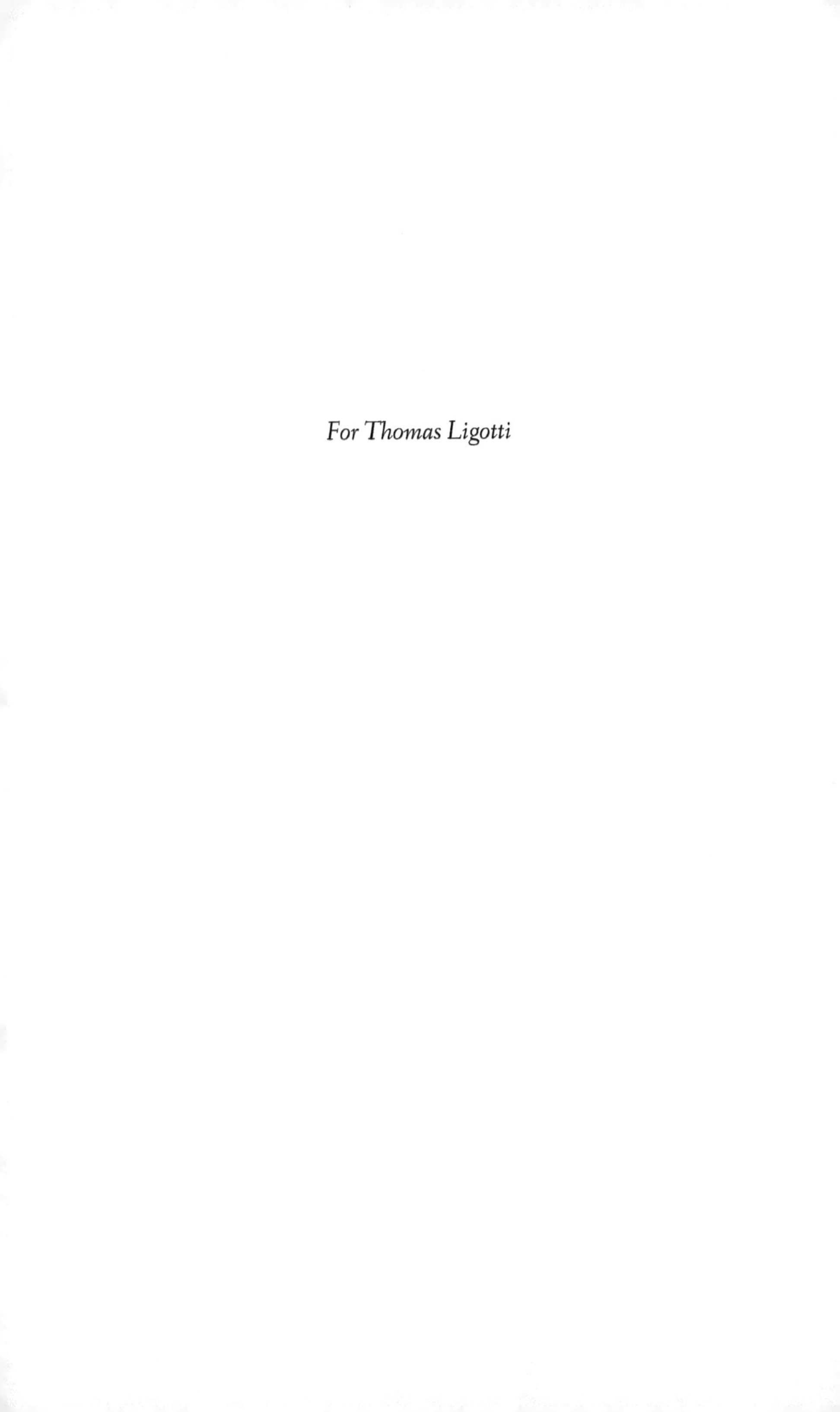

For Thomas Ligotti

BLACK BRANE

MICHAEL CISCO

My foot explodes.

My legs tremble inside their ghostly outlines, under the covers. The pain is pushing me out of moment-to-moment; I can't follow it. The musical drone of voices and birdsongs keep reopening space, and screams begin and end on the black brane. Pain in my unblemished legs, the serene, momentless gaze pours out of my eyes and down my body again. Why does it ever stop?

Voices from the next room...a muffled metallic thudding... and one cricket, chirping listlessly.

No one comes in here. There's nothing I can do—I can barely think. The pain is constant enough that there's no point in trying. Even the pain is tired. Whenever, by chance, it intensifies again, it rises sluggishly and stops short, and I'm too worn out to stifle my feeble groaning. My legs hurt without any apparent cause; there's no discoloration or swelling, no damage, no bullet hole, only shooting pains from hip to heel, and a left foot that might as well have a nail through it. An invisible nail in an invisible wound. Pain that nothing can touch, no matter what I'm given.

My life isn't in danger—this will pass, but I don't know that I believe it. Everything else is just everything else, a dream. I've been benched. I'm out. Life goes on without me. This damp, tangled bed is it. But the black brane is out there, humming. All the strings begin and end on the black brane. I don't know if they *all* do. I just say that and think that because I can't imagine anything different. The pain in my foot won't let me.

As I lie here, I wonder—I don't know if I've ever seen this place from the outside. I mean, I think I have. I think...but I'm not sure. I can't really see it, imagine or remember it. Maybe it has no outside. Maybe it's all inside.

The murmur still trembles in the wall. Filigree of bird song outside. I'll cling to that, if I can. That happy sound, better than words. Even if they are screams of pain or fright, they are happy sounds to me. Pain doesn't give me any rights, but it does put me beyond rights. No one can bicker with me about what a bird sounds like. I would turn the bickering into more song.

Now it's time to confront the "great puzzle": how to get out of bed to go to the bathroom when you can't bend your knees. Roll over onto your stomach first. Turning to the left would hurt. Turn to the right and you'll tumble onto the floor. Heave yourself to the left, and hurt, and then turn face down. Now, pivot around, stiff as a board, like the hands of a clock, until your legs project into space off the bed's edge, and lower them. When your feet have some kind of purchase on the ice-cold floor, press yourself upright. Don't throw yourself over backwards, though!

You're standing.

Now the crutches. Make your way to the door. Pull it toward you. There's a shard of glass impaling your left foot. That's how it feels. Your right foot looks no different from your left. The door hits your crutch. Shift weight, move the crutch clear. The bathroom door is too narrow to pass through abreast, so you have to slide yourself through it sideways, get far enough inside to clear the door. Shut it. (I'm not an animal. Even if there's no one around, I shut the door like a human.) Now turn. Lift the lid. Set aside the crutches so you can remove your robe. Don't fall. Now drop your trousers, hold on to the sink and press your other hand against the wall. Collapse onto the frosty seat. Pray it doesn't break!

I have to sit down to piss, I can't manage it standing. It's making its way out now, through all the kinks and cul de sacs. It'll be a while. I stare at the hexagons. My mouth is open and I sway back and forth a little for wretchedness' sake, my skin tearing with goosebumps in the draft from the open window.

Frozen bathroom light, bathroom air, laced with the smell of industrial cleanser.

Smells filter in from outside, through the inexplicably open window of chicken-wired glass. A faint odor of wood smoke. Children shouting somewhere far away, some afternoon fun, mingling with my own panting. A botanical smell, an herbal smell, something pungent, and buttery, and sweet. I keep sniffing for more of that one. What is it? It's a flower. The kind of little white flowers, I think, that used to grow all over. Sitting on a cold white pot, meagerly piss, shiver, my legs stuck out in front of me, shake. Draw a breath that wavers. Sniff the air. That perfume, the flower I mean, no one ever envied or reproduced it, but that honey-like smell makes me think of something I never could entirely place in my memory.

I was a boy. I went to some performance outside. I was with a school group, I think. Had a crush, as always, and she was there. I never went to any such place, though—it's as if my imagination is, with perfect goodwill, trying to assist my memory by making stuff up. Down a green slope toward a ring of hay bales, encircling a low, bare place where the performance will happen, maybe an Elizabethan play or something, and, on the far side, a palisade of slender green trees, and green gloom, somber and lovely, deepening back into something like a dream, and all the air filled with a fragrance of grass, sun-baked pine needles, peppery eucalyptus, sweetly musty hay, and those buttery, pungent, sour little white flowers.

I'm panting more. There's another pain now. A kind of hope. My face is strained. I can feel it. There, the slope, my little self jogging there, down to the bales and the other children, see past them to the warm, deep green dimness of tall, white-trunked trees, and the grand canopies of lustrous, tiny leaves floating around sinuous black boughs. The fragrance meshed with the daylight. I breathed it, the light, and floated. Jogged—clumsily of course, but floated too. Sustained by the late afternoon like water. A life so different that it might as well not have been mine, but that memory guarantees is mine, and that I am that boy. But is that boy me? Would he have wanted to be? I see the dingy hexagons, my outstretched legs, the bathroom door, the pitilessly bright light in here, *and* I see the supple shade and luminous hay, oaks and poplars...I hear birdsong, sparrow and wrens, mourning doves and crows, blue jays...children shouting...the fragrance of sweet alyssum, wisteria, sage, and pines.

I can't piss when I try and it tries to piss when I don't want— this pissing's full of shit!

Push down and try to draw your legs under you. Throw your weight to the left and lean on the wall. You can't avoid stepping with the left foot and pain shoves a noise out of your throat, an inchoate yelp that doesn't sound like me. Get your drawers up, quick! Then crutches, staggering back to give the door room to swing. You forgot to flush. Now, sideways. Out the door. Voices are following you. Lunge toward the bed, reach it, turn, drop on your ass, and just as lowering the legs forward while prone is a way to move without any additional pain, then, logically, raising the legs upward while throwing the body back onto the bed will hurt. So, get up again, whimpering with shame and frustration, turn, throw yourself down on your face, and raise the legs. Swing the upper body into alignment and so bring the legs around onto the mattress and drop them at last. The pressure on the knee is bad, but dull. Roll onto your back. Struggle up toward the head of the bed. Everything around me is falling and I am suspended. Sweating, panting.

I, you, I don't know. Just the villain.

I hear voices. They aren't the children's, or not the same. Name? What name? Her name? No telling where I am, not like this. Sometimes it's like home, but not always. Which home? I'm alone, but I can hear voices through the walls and...sort of in space? I'm breathing through my mouth, I feel filthy. The pain in my legs makes me sick, and the sickness oozes out of my pores in a thin paste. Wrens, and mourning doves, and crows. Those little white blossoms mixing their aroma with acrid wood smoke and wild mint, those voices singing out from the other side of my forgetfulness. Falling in time, to the sound of time's own voice I guess. The other side of forgetting; that's not death, and I'm not dying, but time does bring death. It's hard not to think about it, at least a little. The pain won't let me forget my body and that means vulnerable, that means mortal.

I don't know why nothing works for this pain. Now it ebbs, because I'm at rest. It gathers its force for a new assault, and likes to give me a bit of respite, to sharpen the despair when it gets bad again. I want to think I'm getting better, and every time the pain comes back it feels as though it were starting all over again and I'm still at its beginning.

Stare at the blank white expanse of the ceiling, the merciless light there in the middle so ugly, here and there grey strands of clumped spider web wafting like—what? Like deep sea feelers. From the sea bottom. Upside down. The difference between the villain I am now and the villain I was, minus only this pain, is too large; it doesn't make sense that such a small difference should make such a big difference. I'm no good now. I can't even sit in a chair. All I can do is lie down or stagger around a little on my crutches. And I can't read, can't make any effort. I only want to be unconscious—or to move freely, in the impossible, ordinary way. I'm not going to stop living. I'm not going to end my life in a dream.

I watch the ceiling for a while. After I don't know how long, it splits open, and my body has no feeling at all. I spring out and aloft, I see the open horizon from miles up in the air, a dull yellow ribbon separating banks of clouds, the powdery blue of the shadowed landscape down there. Skeins of cloud are banked around an expanse of blazing white, and right in front of me there's a flat cloud like a wafer of semi-transparent ice sailing on a silver over black, indigo with white. Everything I see has a voice and sings, calling, and I feel I'm singing, though I never sing. The sun-billows fall on me in the way that I'm here in the sky, and I can see the gold of that afternoon through time to now, the smell of the flowers rips into me, the halo of filtered light in the dim trees and the bright shades of the other kids, she's in there somewhere, one of them, she's the heart of the dream, swift gossamers darting there in late afternoon shallows, swing on each other, bolt and vanish into clouds bright as furnaces, flash in among the hallowed pools of placid dusk, shouting in the street outside—someone's angry—the crows are cawing. This isn't remembering, is it? It could have been her, or it could have been *her*. Both are dead, and in heaven. Both are in death. Both are heaven.

The black brane is on the other side, beyond, eons in space but in touch just the same, like the black hole at the galactic center that holds the Milky Way together: the vast consumer, galactic arms swinging around the drain and our solar system moving right now with one of those arms. A supergiant black hole moving me all through the same time with the earth, the sun, and most of the innumerable fixed stars in a sky that never changes.

Pain growing again. For some people it's always this way; I hope I can remember that. Not sure why.

Remember the black brane.

I can see myself walking, going nowhere special, and it looks like heaven.

***

I can't get up and get out of here, but I can go away into a daydream. I can make things up in my imagination, fabricate people and situations. I can use my memories, scrambled. I can move adjectives to other nouns, transfer names, combine people, separate elements of one person into many. Places, times, every-thing up for grabs, whatever is best at keeping me from the pain here and now.

For the sake of telling a story, let's say that this is something I'm remembering: up until very recently I was working for Dr. Marilyn Shitansky on her research project about holes. She didn't know about the apostolic relationship I have with the black brane, NGC 1313 X-2. I never did tell her.

We're on hiatus now, probably forever. Yes. Dr. Shitansky

went away alone without telling anybody anything, and we all just sort of shrugged and started sorting out what to do next. The scandal, such as it was, blew over immediately. Nobody remembers it now, I don't think. I certainly never told anyone about it. No one knows I was there. Dr. Shitansky was never mysterious, but she had trouble communicating, she was always a little oblivious, so the fact that I haven't heard from her since doesn't necessarily mean anything serious is going.

Creative remembering. This rules! It helps, it makes me go, I can be with this pain in my legs and stave off wretchedness and groaning. Beats just lying here. I've always told myself stories; it's a familiar old habit and that's a comfort too, or at least it isn't any more trouble, OR WHAT I MEAN IS it's a comfortably familiar trouble. You can start anywhere, anyway. From wretchedness, in my case, I can start.

"You mean from villainy, of course..."

Yes, the villainy of a random life.

Dr. Shitansky had been homeless for years. Every week, she'd purchased a single lottery ticket from the same convenience store, always playing the same numbers. I'm trying to remember now—my memory turns everything into cartoons, though. She reminisced to us once about the night before she won.

"We'd found a doorway, a recessed doorway, deep enough to shelter in completely, maximum shelter available for both myself and for Bas also. There we stayed, for six days—approximately. Circumstances tended to neglect our place in the calendar. It was of maximum importance therefore to make note of every date, every time, and to check and corroborate, for a correct awareness of the time.

"That night was a Wednesday night, into Thursday morning. December 29th, 2021 into December 30th of the same year. It had been raining, and chilly. I remember I was sitting on a milk crate, sitting, in the doorway, thinking, sitting, and looking out, looking down, into a puddle there in the street. A black puddle, a streaked puddle, the streaks were reflected lights. The rain wasn't falling that hard anymore, not at that moment, there were only occasional droplets from the sky, and these would strike the puddle, and divert the reflections momentarily from their positions on the surface of the water, which was thick, thick water. Black and thick, like oil it looked, and the streaks would bend around the droplets as they fell and then snap back, and it made me think of elastic and stars. I wanted to try performing astronomical-style calculations on the alterations of the positions of the reflections produced by the strikes from the rain. I was trying to apply geometry to the surface, thinking I would work it out at first as if the involved positions were all strictly stable, then to take into consideration my viewing angle, and then to begin trying to determine how the deformations of the surface, slightly convex surface, could produce indefinitely regular displacements temporarily of the reflections."

She smiled ruefully.

"It was, needless to say, much too complicated for me to do without pen and paper, but it was diverting sufficiently to imagine the stages of the task and the various ways I could describe the distortions, which would have to involve spatial and temporal variables, both. Then a car drove right through the puddle I was looking at, so that I nearly didn't have enough time to withdraw myself, just avoided getting splashed by that fucker, and there were regular tread grooves left cut in the water which filled in more slowly than I would have expected them to. The old pattern came back. That's when I knew I was going to win."

After everything was said and done, she'd found herself endowed by the state with a fortune of over six hundred million dollars. She immediately enrolled in a graduate program in philosophy at UC Irvine, and lived a modest student's life until she completed her doctorate. Her dissertation was published to considerable acclaim. I wish I could remember what it was. She had no interest in teaching, and maintained that it would be wrong for her to take a paid position away from any candidate who might need the salary. During her time at school, she'd invested her money very astutely, and she used it to establish a small research project, the Temporary Institute for the Study of Holes, or TISH.

Dr. Shitansky had been convinced for a long time that she had a hole in her brain. After she won the lottery, she paid for an MRI that confirmed her intuition. There really was a hole about the diameter of a pencil going all the way through her brain, from high on the middle frontal gyrus on the right side to just above the spine on the left side, straight as a die and perfectly round. The specialists were astounded, and Dr. Shitansky was better known for her peculiar brain than for her academic accomplishments. One neurologist said that it was as if her brain had grown around a rod that had subsequently dissolved without a trace. There was no sign whatever of trauma, and Dr. Shitansky had no recollection of any event that could have produced any noticeable change in her brain at all. She insisted, though, that the hole was not congenital, but acquired, unaccountably. What's more, she claimed that she could think with it: that the hole was capable of generating thoughts and mental experiences of its own accord. These thoughts and experiences, she said, were unmistakably different in character from those that were produced by her brain tissue. I can't remember now if she ever claimed that her lottery numbers, or perhaps the premonition she described, were "hole-originant," as she would put it, but she did ascribe her insight into philosophical questions as the result of a kind feedback between her brain and the hole. Dr. Shitansky decided instead to research the phenomenon of holes in general, hoping to bring to light discoveries that would be pertinent to her own case without being specifically about it.

TISH was located on the campus of a defunct theological school, Emissary Westgate College. It's a sprawling green quad with a fountain and a huge sculpture of mottled black metal in congeries of folded triangles at its center, with a mission-style mansion at one end, and framed by two large classroom blocks like white brutalist honeycombs. Dr. Shitansky leased one of the smaller outbuildings, an auditorium encircled by classrooms. At first sight, I thought it looked like a golden hat box. It sat on a dais next to a murky pond with lethargic koi; the entrance was a heavy, darkly-tinted glass door that opened, in a blast of air-conditioning, onto a cavernous lobby. You broke a seal when you pulled the door silently open, and dry institutional air gushed museum and library smell all over you as you came in.

I'm there to hand in a job application, in person and on paper, as stipulated by the TISH website (since taken down). The lobby is thronged with professionally-dressed people, sitting or standing in dead silence, fumbling with papers pressed against their knees or the wall, trying to fill out the forms. A more self-satisfied group are clustered thickly around the unattended reception desk, and every time one of them peels away to join the line standing along the rounded far wall, their forms complete and held out before them like talismans, someone nearby who has been making do with the arm of a chair, or even the floor, would leap up and seize the vacant spot, the coveted horizontal space to write on. I've already filled out my forms. I go and stand meekly by the curved wall.

I can see the parking lot and the paved walkway leading up to the front of the building framed like a painting in one of the enormous windows. Suddenly, a brand-new European station wagon appears and Dr. Shitansky emerges from the rear passenger seat while the car is still moving and marches down the walkway towards us, followed by Bas. She's large and wide, with a huge blonde head that juts forward on a stout neck; her arms barely move at her sides as she walks. She's wearing a buff-colored suede jacket over a green shirt and white slacks, and wipes her nose with a quick flip of her finger as she mounts the steps to the door. Everyone pivots to look as she whips the door lightly aside; the crowd parts and scatters like a flock of pigeons as she stamps past all of us, eyes riveted to the ground, and vanishes into the corridor.

Her driver, tall and wan with a violently thin red mouth,

appears a moment later, carrying a clipboard. Everyone begins murmuring, tentatively edging in her direction. She walks directly to the reception desk, deftly lifting the counter flap and letting herself into the square.

"Just a minute, just a minute," she says.

She doesn't answer questions, she just gives directions.

"Your A23 forms go in this basket. Your B17 forms go in this basket."

She raises her voice and addresses the room.

"You will have noticed that there are no wastebaskets in this lobby. Any forms you have received here will have to be left here. No one takes any of our forms away. You will be called by name and in order. The answers to any questions you might have can all be found on the forms; I can't tell you anything that isn't already written on the forms."

Without a second glance at anyone, she empties the first basket, sits down at the reception desk, and begins sorting the forms in piles. Whatever sheepishly muttered questions or pleasantries are directed toward her, she ignores.

Suddenly she stands again, takes up her clipboard, raises the flap, and walks over toward those of us who are lined up against the rounded inner wall.

"Which one of you is Gross?"

"Me," I answer, raising my hand.

She waves me after her, through the door and into a broad, evenly-lit hallway with tinted glass wall sections.

"You had better have all your shit," she snaps.

"I have got all my shit," I say.

Striding over to the left she throws open a very wide door made of a single piece of thick, dark hardwood.

"Great—clerical!" she says past me and I enter a grey room, airy and spartan, filled with wan daylight, stripped of color by the smoky windows.

The door closes silently behind me. That was it. How we met.

Dr. Shitansky sits behind a massive desk, also made out of a single slab of polished, heavy hardwood, and completely bare except for two wooden bowls. There are two chairs that were modern design fifty years ago in front of the desk and she indicates one of them, so I sit in it. She's still wearing her jacket. Bas the basenji lies with her chin on the floor in a patch of daylight; a silent, white and brown, small dog with deep velvety furrows in her brow, a red bandana, and a curled tail.

Now Dr. Shitansky is looking at my face. It's like having a huge film camera pointed at me, taking me all in. I try to return her gaze. Her pupils don't seem to need to move; she's sort of fixing me all together, instead of scanning me for details. I notice that one of the bowls is neatly heaped with walnuts. The other one is empty.

"Can you keep a secret?" she asks. "Can you keep your mouth shut about everything we do here, down to the least detail?"

"If you need me to."

She points at me, extending her arm to full length, and stands up.

"I mean not one word, not even about what we eat for lunch, not even that you work here."

"I won't say anything."

Still pointing.

"You married?"

"...No."

"Divorced? Kids?"

I clear my throat.

"—No to both."

She draws air in through her nose, and her nostrils flare. She drops her arm and sits again.

"OK...OK..."

"You have anyone you could talk to? Anyone we would worry about?"

"No, no one."

"Renbrui says you were married. There was a record. How are you not divorced and not married?"

I look her straight in the eye.

"Because she's *dead*."

She pivots, and looks outside. The light bathes her face, her jaw has snapped shut.

"OK, look..." she says.

She doesn't go on. We sit there for a while. Apart from her regular breathing, there's no sound in here at all.

"Show Renbrui your information," she says, and holds out her hand. "I'm sorry about that...that earlier."

I get up and turn to leave, thinking she's gesturing me out the door.

"Thanks," I say.

"You don't shake?" she says, a little indignant.

"Oh!"

She takes my hand between her thumb and the rest of her fingers and gives it one dry jolt up and down.

"Listen," she says. "We shake hands here. Understand?"

"Sure," I say. "Sure, I understand."

"You wear a ring?"

"No, I don't."

"You ever wear one?"

"...Not regularly."

"*Why* haven't you?" She asks me this with some genuine curiosity. Not much, but some.

I shrug, more with my face than with my shoulders.

"I never really thought about it. Seemed a little extravagant, I guess."

I note that she has a ring of pale metal on her left little finger.

"Go get one," she says. "As long as you don't get the Hope diamond, it's on us. Wear it when you next come here. Bring the receipt to Renbrui and she'll get you reimbursed."

"OK, sure. Thanks."

"Tell Renbrui to send in the next applicant. See you," she says.

The door swings weightlessly open and I am back out in the

hallway, where the air conditioning lightly tosses the fronds of the potted rubber plants.

In the lobby the tall, pale woman...Renbrui...is talking with one of the men. She looks up at me, breaks off her conversation unceremoniously and comes over, waving me back through the doors and into the hall again.

Without seeming at all sickly or weak, she is the palest person I've ever seen. She has a huge mane of regularly curled black locks shot through with grey, falling down and mantling her shoulders. She wears a short jacket of dark red velvet over a dark purple shirt, a floral scarf around her neck, and black trousers. Her eyes are startlingly blue, with a deep crease under each one.

"Did she ask you to buy anything?" Renbrui asks, once the doors are shut.

"A ring. Anything but the—"

"—the Hope diamond, right. Give me your shit and go for a walk. Don't wait in the lobby. Come back in twenty minutes. You're not carrying a phone are you?"

"No."

That had been one of the stipulations. No cellular phones on TISH premises.

"Then how are you going to know it's been twenty minutes?"

I pull my wristwatch out of my jacket and show it to her. Without pulling it from my hands, she turns it this way and that. I get a whiff of her perfume. It's the same as my fourth grade teacher's.

"Nice," she says, eyes on the watch, which has hands.

"Come back when that says 3:18."

I step out into sunshine and birdsong. I look in the koi pond. They have a way to slip over and around each other, staring and mouthing, through the semi-transparent dark green fronds of shapeless pond growth glued to the black bottom of the pond, spotted with livid copper pennies people chucked in with their wishes.

With no special impulses, and not knowing the place, I wander over to the sidewalk with my eyes on the pavement, thinking about not stepping on cracks. That old bit of business comes back to me all the way from childhood too, when I would calculate whether or not it made more sense to step on every single crack with the idea that this would drain the curse of its efficacy. My mother's back would be at risk in the short term, but if she could hold out then she'd be set for life once I'd stepped on enough cracks—unless the curse had a way to restore itself...A Mexican Goth kid dressed like Heaven 17 passes me. The wind stirs a little in his earring and I turn the corner and walk past soccer practice. It's been ten minutes. Cars whoosh past me.

Turn off onto a footpath, a cocoa-colored scar in green and tan grass linking the sidewalk to a paved causeway or whatever. Steam table smell from the cafeteria, which is an angular white skeleton with black windows and a futuristic raised patio, umbrella tables with built-in benches. Coffee and eggs, toast, stale sausage...

Turn the corner and close in on TISH again, pooled in the shade of tall old trees, a veil of soccer dust in the air. Back up the steps to the front door. The pale woman with the clipboard, Renbrui, is back at the receptionist desk, now cleared of applicants. She looks up as I come in and remains seated, her pen poised on hiatus over her paperwork.

"You're hired," she says. "We'll need you here at 1 PM starting Monday. You can do that?"

"No problem."

She stands up.

"Which of you is Diop?"

In order to maintain maximum control over the project, Dr. Shitansky banned computers and computer-like devices from the Institute. All TISH business was conducted on official letterhead, every sheet of which came with a unique serial number. We were forbidden to discard any paperwork, no matter how trivial. Managing this waste paper was my chief responsibility; our version of "File 13" was a pretty sizeable interior room, which had a skylight but no windows, filled with old, battered filing cabinets. That was a separate archive from the currently viable document horde, which was kept in an identical room across the hall. Every morning, Renbrui would unlock both of these rooms in my presence, and my desk was situated smack dab in the middle of the corridor, right between them, where I could keep an eye on both doors at all times. Renbrui would come by and lock them again during my lunch breaks, as well as before and after my daily rounds collecting everyone's waste paper to bring back to File 13. Then, of course, she would lock up for the night at 5 PM sharp, whether I was there or not.

I had two blocky old telephones on my desk. The beige phone was for internal calls only and had no exterior connection; everybody in TISH had one of these, with a row of transparent, cubical call buttons below the main keypad. I was one of the only employees to have a second telephone—a black one—that was connected to the local network via landline, as well as to a primeval answering machine that looked like old military hardware. The thing was fascinating: a squat, gunmetal-grey box with the word "ANSAFONE" emblazoned on it in the kind of cursive metal type that you'd normally see on the exteriors of old fifties' cars. The console consisted of a huge black on-off switch, a black volume knob with a white radius indicator notched on top, a red power light surrounded by a discreet metal collar, a yellow light marked "absent," a heavy incremental switch that could be set to "erase," "listening," "confirm," or "message" (the yellow "absent" light was tucked confusingly in between "listening" and "confirm"), another red light labelled "tape end," and a big black button underneath it that said "test button." There was no manual for the ANSAFONE, and the manufacturer was long out of business, so I had to dumb out how it worked on my own. The old tapes were shot, so Dr. Shitansky, who seemed to find the machine as intriguing as I did, ordered bespoke reels from an answering machine enthusiast and refurbisher in South Korea. Any time we received an incoming call, I was not to answer it, but to record it while listening, and transcribe it on official letterhead. The call had to be entered in a log, and the message would then be passed on to Dr. Shitansky. If she had a reply to give, she would type it up and give it to me, on letterhead, to be read back by return call, also logged. The black telephone was not to be used for any other reason, barring an emergency.

All of this gear had been found heaped up behind some boxes of miscellaneous supplies in a closet near the old box office. At first, I used one of the old electric typewriters that came with the building, but it was so curse-inducingly cranky and unreliable that Renbrui took pity on me and sent me out to get a new antique one, from a vetted dealer. It could be electric, but not electronic, that is, it couldn't have anything like a memory. No equipment in the building was allowed to have a memory. That of course meant no copy machines—I had to use carbons. Those were no breeze to find, either.

Then there was the library. Since we were off the web, this ruled out instant research. For that matter, employees were also forbidden to look up any online information relevant to TISH activities away from the Institute either. It was my job to stock and maintain the library, which occupied two walls of the auditorium. We had encyclopedias and general reference works; those I was free to order fresh from my home computer. Anything more specific, though, had to be purchased through one of two Shitansky-approved dealers, and I had to go ask for the books in person, supplying a list on our own letterhead that I was not permitted to relinquish. The dealer had to fill the order in my presence. In addition to collecting the books and stocking the shelves, I had to track who was looking at which book when and make sure every book was present and accounted for at the end of each day. Even the notes people took while consulting the books had to be on official letterhead and kept in lockboxes when not out for use during the day. Then there was all the HR personnel paperwork, too. I had to manage the tax documents and insurance stuff, all on paper, and laboriously explain to the various authorities and agencies involved that we did zero online anything, repeating phrases like "that's not Institute policy," and "we have a strict all hard copy protocol" over and over again.

TISH is just a loose confederation where everybody's improvising their own hole-related, idiosyncratic projects. You can do whatever you want, so long as Dr. Shitansky gets to see your results. So there are as many research angles and topics as there are researchers, about half a dozen. (That means half a dozen small research libraries merged into one, all by me.) In addition to Dr. Shitansky, Renbrui, Bas, and me, there was Allegre the engineer, Dr. Liu the string physicist, Daladara, an occultist who was always off somewhere, a linguist named Corngholm, and a remote neurologist named Dr. Memon who would answer specific questions by ciphered correspondence that I had to decode using a latter-day Enigma type box that Allegre built for us. I made the rounds daily, collecting and distributing stacks of manila folders, starting with Daladara, since he was never around. Allegre would be in his shop working on something Dr. Shitansky had ordered, and there was this enormous machine he was working on; it looked like the boiler off a locomotive. He told me all about it, but I couldn't make head nor tail of his explanation, beyond the fact that it was supposed to be a new kind of generator. Corngholm was another phantom. He bicycled some enormous distance to work every day and so he was usually towelling off and changing out of his ergonomic aerodynamic sports gear when I came by. Next to his desk, he had a work table that was covered with a neat grid of index cards, some of which were inscribed with short phrases, the rest blank. He was creating a temporal overview of the concept of holes, and where there were concurrent results he would stack index cards on top of each other.

The table was marked along the top and left edges, giving the cards two axes in time somehow. I didn't make any effort to understand what he was doing. Wilson would be smoking and doodling, usually, with a little transistor radio playing. Even though it involved adding switchbacks, I plotted my route so it would end with Dr. Liu, because I enjoyed talking with her. She was an older woman with big glasses and a bulky denim jacket; she had a gift for describing complicated physics to a curious layman like myself, which meant she had patience as well as fluency, and she never initiated an explanation herself. I'd ask what she was working on at the moment, or if there was anything interesting going on, and only then would she drop her hands into her lap, pivot her chair toward me, and begin. When I'd ask a question, she'd give one long swooping nod and answer it succinctly and clearly. I always left her company feeling a little brightened up.

After the mail round, the day would begin a steady dilation, opening out into a rapt vacancy that might have been humming with possibilities. Alone at my desk in the hall, I'd bang on the typewriter and monitor the ANSAFONE, get up to file or discard or retrieve more carbons. It was a little like working in the nave of a church. Every sound went flying away down the broad, empty hall before and behind me, toward the green fronds that wavered behind the tinted glass where the corridor banked off to the right, some thirty feet from the front of my desk. The air duct above me whispered ceaselessly, belching cool dry library air down my back and over my shoulders, resting there like a pair of steadying hands. From time to time, I'd detect the sound of a human voice coming through the walls. The various members of the Institute were encouraged to work together on joint experiments, but for the most part everyone was creating their own individual projects with an eye to linking them together later. I don't know what Dr. Shitansky thought about this, but for her own part she seemed to be doing the same, spending a great deal of time poring over Levinas' essay "On Escape" and taking notes in a thick ledger that I had to lock up every night, with Renbrui there to ensure there was no peeking.

—Me again.

Not *me* again. I don't want it.

Someone doesn't.

—There's a languid play of sunbeams. Each is a timeless scream of anguish, terror, and loss. A beautiful grief-light whose beams trail like aquatic fronds, shedding dignity down on the suffusion ground. The pain isn't intense but it is mercilessly persistent. Even when I don't feel it, it's there, momentarily balked and come around the other side. I want to remember, I think. The memories are flying. Not me. No, don't want to remember. We fought in the kitchen. Her face shouting down at me, that last time.

Waking up in the dark, not knowing how long it's been since some other time, when I was last here, paying attention I mean. The dark, which must have developed in the typical, gradual way, is for me suddenly here, right now. I drifted into it without moving. There's a line of clear light far up on the wall, serrated along the top and flat along the bottom, shaped like the aperture that admitted it I guess.

Listening in the dark, I hear sweet sounds, like chimes, gemmed foil opening in little flowerets, drop into churning, syrupy sound, in a trembling, uncertain beginning. What am I hearing? Is it coming from inside me? Opening out, onto a vast, motionlessly undulating medium, clinking with spiral, bubbling flourishes/ A rush and soar that sweeps along sea-cries of child-like life, raises billows that hum and frosted surf rolling over warm, softly-beading ice. I hear the swell and ebb of glass lungs, an impersonal choir of totemic voices. The breath writhes down, seething pebbles beneath dawn thrum, a whinny, something turns steadily in place with a shifting channel shoaling over it, a vertical shudder springs, a sinuous whine pealing. The turning starts to tumble in two lobes. A projectile grates against the air and crashes next to me, so that I flinch and call out in pain as my legs spasm. I keep my eyes closed and listen. Something is and isn't happening, like a waking dream that isn't mine.

It's hard. I can almost hear the shouting from the kitchen. Launched at my face, those words. All true. I listen, latching on to sound, to block out what she says.

The tumbling flares outgas a plaintive cry that sets a coppery mesh hissing against a stone panel, the strength swells and another whistling mortar arcs toward me, with another close behind, trailing swiftly-fading chorded echoes. The tumble begins to lope along, and there's a muted gibbering from the next room. I hear a homely refrain being whistled, very familiar, while the loping climbs over brightly jagged and resonant sobs, then stands still, wonders, reconsiders, insists. As the whistling irregularly dwindles out of hearing, ghostliness folds itself like northern lights on the other side of the wall, the insistence fades, and now there's inchoate, expectant transitioning that's all siphons of streaks and deep tollings that dart and retract.

Then wriggling into silence that feels temporary, very ready to stop. Leaning way out, away from—never mind from what— just away from, and toward all the sources currently hidden in the gloom, all the sources of sound, all this to tell me there's no end to how full of shit I always am. That's NGC 1313 X-2, the black brane, telling me. I feel like I'm rolling through mysterious dioramas I can't see, and the mystery isn't how I think of it. There's no pointed, deliberate investigation, no cool; just groping in sounds and colors for something to see and name and a way to link what I see to me and what's around me, even if it's only enough to call it "whatever," and get situated. Hearing and feeling all this, while all I really can see is the white ceiling dimmed in the slate-grey glow of the night outside. I haven't got a reason to say that; everything that's happening to me right now comes from the black brane, and I don't have an explanation for that idea. I tell myself I know, but I can't prove it to myself or figure out why I tell myself that.

Instead I weld myself to the idea that this is the evidence; the mystery of NGC 1313 X-2, the black brane, is that the idea is inexplicably there, in my mind I mean, so that I want to believe it's the secret of pain trying to help me understand, back in there, the surface where I go when I dream. That old game of dabbling fingers in dreams. Poke through them like the heap of clothes a prisoner or hospital inmate drops in a pile on the counter, idly scanned for clues that lead to other clues that lead to still other clues and it's nothing but clues about clues on and on. My leg keeps kicking. What does that mean? Does that mean something? A steady gout hand gives the long screw through my left foot a good firm twist and tug, a nerve streak flares up my leg—another fine clue.

—Dr. Liu—I should explain—Dr. Liu told me that string theorists call black holes "black branes." A brane is where the strings begin and end. The black brane has its own horizon. It hurts. The black brane is not a point in space like a black hole. It hurts it's a more elaborate structure. Not just a point. Nobody's ever seen one outside math equations. It collects strings, in particular the ends of strings. It hurts it collects string ends so some strings get caught at both ends and form loops. I don't think they can get free. I think once they're stuck they're stuck for good, inside that horizon. I know there's a black hole or black brane in the center of the it hurts galaxy, and what it holds holds something that holds something else and so on in a chain that ultimately includes the sun, earth, and me. All dragging after the rotation of the black brane. The black brane isn't my brain or any brain, which is to say, poor translator that I am, that I'm talking about myself, and not even saying anything, but it hurts there is a confrontation that involves me, and what confronts me doesn't notice me. Not by chance, though, it hurts, it isn't a coincidence, I know the black brane is collecting *my* strings. Dr. Liu said that a brane has something called a worldvolume. The black brane has a worldvolume it hurts it has me in its worldvolume and it makes me vibrate with it, snarling me up so I'm tangled in it, transformed into its apostle with nothing to see, no message to teach or revelations to proclaim. It's something nothing escapes; heaven's absence staring down, all darkness and can't stop its thoughts; impotent collector of life, nothing but a sop, it hurts, a halo without a head and a voice all trembled out of shape. Don't you think if I were talking about death, pain, or sorrow, I'd just call them that instead of getting coy with symbols? I talk about the black brane—you tell *me* why.

All I know is, it's not a hole. It hurts. It's a surface with a structure in a whole assortment of dimensions, just a candy dish and a sampler of these tiny dimensions tucked in around the big ones. But I never believed in dimensions. There's only time to believe in. Whatever it hurts we're talking about should just be time...

The black brane is a time of its own; my time passively goes into it and becomes its time, so my time's not mine. The halo wants my head. It wants to make a witness. Like a predatory sainthood zeroing in on me. It wants my shouted-in face, marked with everything she said. It's telling me that if you call out in distress to be saved then this is what answers, reaching right down from pure snowy starlight to my bed, sour with sweat, and me glued to it slack-mouthed and staring, and night's darkness is just its transparency. Don't tell me anything. My glasses are lying next to me; the illuminated light switch on the far wall is a tiny peach-pink latticed sun with sunspots and needle-like flares to my nearsighted eyes. The room relaxes and expands, instantly widening by hundreds of millions of miles, becomes a solar system of glints, faint patches of light, the wan astral cloud here in the foreground is the bed, with magma chained up beneath in rocks so tight it can't bubble, can't even budge, heat immobilized under a stone lid and a wispy sheet of ice.

Where is everyone? They've all disappeared. The black brane ate them. Now I disappear too. But I won't be joining them. Whatever passes the event horizon and falls into the black brane, falls alone. Whoever is linked to me, leaves. That is, they fall into events, and away from me. The event horizon is the point at which "away" becomes eternal; always farther and farther and farther. You wouldn't believe how far we can fall apart from each other.

What night is this? Is this another night? I don't know what night it is. I just know I'm going to have to get up. That is, I'm going to have to lever myself upright and onto those crutches, and then make my way to the sink. My mouth is so dry it almost hurts. No, wait—I filled a water bottle...Please let it be here, let there be some...

I drink. I'm not sure it helps, but it's a change. I'm still in pain, but also numb. For the moment, leaden resignation. I remember Ernie Allegre, the engineer, after he burned his hand. It was all bandaged, and he sits there on the bench outside TISH, beneath a huge tree with a pale brown trunk, the bark grows in shreds, I couldn't tell you what kind of tree it is, but he sits under it, with its long willowy leaves spinning, his bandaged hand healing on his knee, and there's a dangerous, sullen expression in his eyes. He hates healing almost as much as he hates getting hurt. He feels cheated. How did he do it? He was working on the decoherence reactor and something overheated, fell off and landed on his hand, burned it, burned it good. I heard his howl reverberating down the Institute's long, silent hallways.

Dr. Shitansky was concerned that someone might check our electricity meter and read the peaks somehow, then use that information to figure out what she was up to. She wanted to get off the grid, and Daladara suggested that the meter might have been able to pick up any "electromagnetic field activity," as he called it, so the Institute should be shielded throughout. He's always thinking of things like that, farfetched vulnerabilities. He's like a pioneer, constantly pushing back the frontiers of new vulnerabilities. So Dr. Shitansky wanted a power source built in situ, so nobody could sneak any recording gizmos into it, and, also at Daladara's suggestion, she said the power supply had to operate on principles related to the research it was powering. So Allegre, who had already been hired to build the hole winch, the zero matrix, and other contraptions that Dr. Shitansky needed, came up with the decoherence reactor.

Dr. Liu explained it to me. Water is poured into a closed chamber inside the reactor, where it falls by chance into one of two channels. One channel empties into a boiler that vents the water as steam into the reactor chamber, while the other channel vaporizes the water mechanically, like a perfume atomizer, then vents the vapor into the reactor chamber after passing it through a heated duct that brings it to the same approximate temperature as the steam. So, you have two different sources for steam coming into the reactor chamber, but the vents are connected and randomized so that it isn't possible for any observer to tell which steam originates from the boiling process and which originates from the vaporization process. It's a law of physics, though, that two different states cannot evolve into the same state, because, as physicists put it, "information cannot be destroyed." The information, in this case, is the cause of the transformation from water into water vapor. Since there are two possible causes, and these two causes are indiscernible—at least, for a human observer—the reactor creates the semblance of a destruction of information.

"The information isn't really destroyed," she says. "But, it is threatened. The reactor puts pressure on the information, puts it at risk of being destroyed, in order to amplify the information's reactive auto-defense field in something we're calling a 'reciprocal disjunctive synthesis reaction.' Quite a mouthful, I know! The pushback from the information as it resists being destroyed is a harnessable energy source that can be used to do work. It takes the form of a kind of tremor in the foil lining of the reactor chamber—"

(She wiggles her pinched fingers in the air to show the tremor.)

"—which agitates magnets that in turn generate electric power, some of which is rerouted back into running the reactor, while the rest can be used in our experiments."

So, a power source for the Institute. Once Allegre got it working, we were able to run individual experiments off the reactor. Once his hand healed, he installed solar panels too, and with those we were able to run the whole Institute without needing any connection to the grid. A weird silence settled over the building from that point on. I could feel it warp around me whenever I placed my foot on the first step leading up to the front entrance, and it released me, a little reluctantly, when I left at night. Then the whoosh and roar of the city found me again, but it only seemed loud compared to the uncanny quiet inside. Once I stepped to and fro, feeling the tingling snap closed around me and then pop open again, the noise dwindle almost instantly to nothing, then flare back up again. That was some fun.

We all speak in hushed tones inside TISH now, even Renbrui. The reactor, though, makes faint musical sounds that neither Allegre nor anyone else can trace back to any cause. You have to be right alongside the reactor to hear them, and they keep altering. When I first listened, I heard a sound like a puff of air humming in a large PVC pipe. It was a brief noise, but it repeated randomly a few times, and sometimes it echoed, as if the sound had bounced off a tall cliff and travelled back to me across a great open space. Sometimes the echo was distinct, and at other times it squelched, fell flat with a noise like a shoe scuffing a thin carpet. Wherever it came from, the echo had no relation to the acoustics of the room housing the reactor; the sound seemed to waft in through the walls, or drop down from the air below the high ceiling.

Dr. Liu told me she'd heard a different sort of sound, a harmonious sound.

"If I were any kind of musician, I could try to play it on a piano," she says, smiling.

She described a sound that went through a few different harmonies, always toward the low end of the scale. It had what she calls a powdery, blurry timbre, and it cut in and out, she says, sort of like a car radio signal whipping in and out when you pass through a series of short tunnels. These sounds hang in space when you hear them, and there's nothing to connect them to the reactor except proximity; you only hear them when you're right by the reactor. So, how could I have heard them just now, in my bed here? Allegre studied plans and maps of the campus, wondering if the noises might be caused by some machinery in a forgotten underground tunnel or storage room, but the ground beneath TISH is solid; Emissary Westgate has never had any underground tunnels. He then began to consider the situation of the room in the building and relative to other buildings, thinking that it might be a natural acoustic focal point, like a whispering gallery. If it were, then the sounds we've been hearing might come from the other side of campus, or even from miles away, and might travel via an unbroken series of fortuitously positioned sonic mirrors.

Of all of us, Daladara is the most interested in the sounds; Allegre keeps shooing him out of the reactor room, where he likes to camp out and listen. He's been around more, and I've been getting to know him. He won't say what he thinks the sounds are or what they mean, if anything. He just sits there with his head craned, rapidly flicking his abacus and taking notes. The reactor is about the size of a small car, covered in gleaming black tiles, with a thicket of copper pipes on top. They all lead into a central chamber that protrudes from the body of the machinery like a conning tower with a petalled trumpet-bell smokestack emerging from its side. Standing in front of the reactor, the opening inside the elliptical bell is perfectly black, like a window on nothing. The resonation foils are extended out from around the reactor chamber up inside those petals, as I understand it, and they have to have space around them in order to work. I guess this means the dark space is a receptacle for invisible vibrations. It's hard not to think of it alternately as the eye, ear, or mouth of the reactor; that perfectly-delineated dark spot has a way to track you. The custodians like to pretend they're about to empty their trash right into the opening, trying to get a rise out of Allegre, or whoever happens to be there. I've seen one or another of them do it at least five times. They never seem to get tired of it; like all their antics. Everything they do, all their little japes and funny expressions, strike me as almost tiresomely familiar even the first time I see them, are perverse by the first repetition, and invisible by about the fourth or fifth.

The Institute has an amazing contingent of custodians. There must be at least ten, but I've never seen more than four at a time. They come in any shape color and size but they all look alike somehow, not so much because they all have to wear the same nameless blue garment, but mainly because they act alike, never taking anything seriously, or not for very long. The custodians work constantly. They're always around, the tip of the tongue poking out the side of the mouth, a cigarette behind the ear, polishing the gleaming floors, replacing working light bulbs and fluorescents, washing crystal-clear windows, carefully oiling the utterly silent doors.

I'm still wearing the ring I bought. Dr. Shitansky did stipulate that it had to be a new ring, bought new by me and worn by no one else. A plain, slim band of steel fits neatly into the old groove around the base of my left ring finger. Now, I find I can't remember whether or not we were told to keep our rings on all the time, or only at work, keeping at least a part of each of us always in a hole, so to speak. Somehow I got the notion that we were going to be asked to remove and contemplate the holes in our rings at certain times, but "hole time" was never announced. The raised, ungleaming band between the bevels is minutely scored with a grain that looks like fine hair combed flat, while the bevels themselves are smooth and reflective as glass. That squashed, shapeless, ugly blotch there is my own tiny reflection, as though another me were peeping out through this odd circular slot in reality at the bed-ridden old villain he is. He might be puzzling over the connection between us, but, considering how beaten out of shape and trampled he is, it's plenty clear to me. An excellent likeness, if not a photographic one.

There were cheaper rings—I could have probably gotten away with wearing a plastic ring out of a bubble gum dispenser, if there were any anymore. I chose this ring because I felt it was not undignified, not vainglorious, and above all because it communicated no impression, and so gave nothing away. Distinctive dress is too telling, too conspicuous. It's vitally important that I keep to a half-light, to hide my shame. Hiding villainy I'm ashamed of, but as well hiding a blazing spotlight of shame itself. No spots on me. Look at me, don't see me, above all don't watch me. Let me be only words on a page without a face or a voice, and even that is unbearable, but I know myself well enough by now—to my cost!—to know that any silence I try to keep will only break that much more loudly later on.

There was one day I had a copy of Creation Rebel's *Starship Africa* on vinyl with me for some reason, and suddenly Dr. Shitansky catches a glimpse of it.

"What's that?" she asks, pointing.

The record cover shows an eclipse viewed from space.

"This? This is dub," I say.

When she continues staring at me interrogatively I go on, feeling very stupid and self-conscious.

"Dub is a kind of music from Jamaica. It's reggae bass and drums with a lot of space around them, and snatches of vocals or melody, guitar or melodica, horns, that sort of emanate and echo in and out on top of the rhythm. This one's a classic."

"Have we got a record player?"

"No," Renbrui says instantly.

"Get a record player. I want to hear that."

Of course she wants to listen to records: they all come with a hole in them. Except CDs do too. And tape cassettes have two holes. All those ways of recording sound are just so many spirals around so many holes, spun out of speaker holes, spun into ear holes, and etching themselves, lost wax-style, into a smooth patch of ready brain, ready to be forgotten so I can remember them later, note by note, inflection by inflection.

Dr. Shitansky and Bas turn to go and Renbrui in the same moment marches up to me, putting out her hand. I pivot the record into it. She tucks the album under her arm and strides away. They're so well-coordinated. Renbrui is like an extension of Dr. Shitansky's will, but, if anything, this only reflects Rebrui's greater, more exciting kind of power. Romantic feelings about Renbrui anyway, neatly set aside by me into the "do not act" channel. A foolhardy dream to clash with her reserve, like the clash of shields...legendary shields.

<hr>

I have to go through a stack of VHS recordings of Dr. Shitansky discussing some of her ideas and transcribe them. The videos often come with a date onscreen somewhere, but they are numbered in an order that doesn't follow the chronology of the recordings.

Dr. Shitansky sitting in a dingy classroom someplace, with a half-swabbed whiteboard behind her. It looks a little as if she were directing a seminar, except there's no table—and no coughing or rustling either, nothing to indicate the presence of anyone else except Bas, who is lying with her chin on the floor. She's already seated when the tape starts with a fizzle of static and the image resolves; someone else had been there to start the camera I guess. She's already talking.

She says: "Everything that exists..." and then stares at

nothing for about ten seconds while she raises her hand slowly, index finger up, pointing toward the ceiling.

"...comes out of a hole," she says finally.

She relaxes, lowering her hand. The chair has no arms, so her hand just drops to her side. Her brow furrows and she lets her breath out, a bit tired. Then she rallies, gathering her discursive powers for another foray.

"Holes retrieve...and retain...what appears to be lost."

Her eyes are fixed on a spot somewhere above, and she's talking to herself, not to anyone in the room.

"It's important...to distinguish between a hole and what I call...what I call a cavity...A cavity is a hole *in* something, that is to say, it's a feature of the...substance in which it arises, or is lowered."

Each statement is a kind of gambit, an attempt to capture something that never quite stops in place long enough to be seen, but that leaves traces of itself behind. Then she tries again, from a different angle each time.

"When you study a cavity," she goes on, "you're studying the material the cavity is in, that holds—that's holding, the cavity. You don't see a hole there...You don't see the hole, you see the...omission, or deterioration, in the material that the cavity is...is in, is bored into. So for example if hypothetically you were to go into a cave or a mine, what is there to study? You look at the walls, you study the rocks, you're doing geology or industrial engineering or mining engineering, but the one thing you're not studying is the hole itself. How do you study a hole as a hole?"

Renbrui appears around the corner.

"Shitansky says find her more dub."

"Uh, ok, sure...Oh!—On expense, right?"

"Yeah on expense," she says offhandedly, passing me on her way to somewhere else as always. "And on vinyl. Don't forget."

Evidently Dr. Shitansky finds *Starship Africa* fascinating, and in some way relevant to her studies. She wanted LPs for the minimal electronics I guess. No dub on Edison cylinders, too bad. That would be something. Through the rustle of the wax, the silence and patience of the music as it reaches out into vacancy and makes it ring; a good-humored explorer of a haunted void, making itself at home. Music radar navigating in the dark, returning distorted, half-remembered voices that shape trembling words from the other side.

Flat on my back. Pain at low tide. That moon is going to raise it. Just now, what I wouldn't give for a little draft of air. Push aside the stale brown gelatin that clings to me and give me just one cool lungful of something breathable. I'd hold it. The cool from it would blue me from the lung frames out, slide down my arms and legs, unlacing me, nerve by nerve, escape me to heaven.

No such luck, though. Just pull after pull of dead fumes.

I sit up without meaning to, abruptly, and for a moment I fear the answering spasm in my leg will burst out into a new blaze of pain. No, it's petering out again, but did I hear that? A baffled groan through the walls and floors? Of pain? Not mine?

Nothing to hear but the whine of my tinnitus, my own open mouth foully panting, and the distant sigh of whatever is living out there beyond the walls. This sound was certainly within the walls, and it was pain I heard. Is there someone else in pain here?

There are some handwritten diatribes from Dr. Shitansky's battered manila folders to be typed up. This yields some further revelations about her research. The idea that everything in existence comes from holes is the conceptual spinal cord. Space is a hole, for example, but space is time, according to Einstein, which means time is a hole with space, not in space. There's a lot here about time. She says that Einsteinian physics reduces time to a dimension of space—3d+1 she calls it, looks like D&D —but that's wrong and every dimension of space is also or somehow moreso, according to her, a dimension of time, or rather all the dimensions are encompassed by time as the vaster aspect of existence. It looks like she's trying to think of objects and the space around and between them as "time-statues," and she kind of toys with signifying the demotion of space in her scheme by calling it "room" instead of space.

I think what she says here is that she thinks of time as being like a hole that everything comes out of, like the future is a hole the present comes out of and the past is a hole it goes into. They aren't the same holes, though, and the present is a "dual-hole" because the future drains into it and the past drains out of it. Over here she says past tense is "prior-hole" and future tense is "post-hole," while the present is "hole-reciprocal."

These notes are about Levinas. She says that what he calls the Other is another hole, and she drew an arrow back to the big capital O of Other, like that orthographic coincidence is evidence of her being on to something. I mean, it's not spelled with an O in French. The Other has to be a hole, that is, an opening that things come out of, instead of what she calls here a "cardboard cut-out," a projection that blocks out the "hole-intentness" of the Other. Dr. Shitansky says every individual person has a basic drive to be the only hole in most situations, and so they don't want to deal with other holes. Everyone's plastering over all the other holes with cardboard cut-outs and interacting with them instead. Reminds me of Ellison. Levinas keys ethics in to interacting with the Other hole-to-hole, so to speak.

Now, these notes over *here* are about artistic innovation, new discoveries in science and so on, also coming out of holes, but, in addition, bringing some of their "hole-essence" along with them: injecting their fields or artistic media or communities with a kind of aroma or ambience of the hole. It's like a kind of novelty-energy that prompts further "exlaboration" and "collmunicativity." I got lost typing these up, I admit.

Anyway, Dr. Shitansky has a whole sheaf of notes that seem

to repeat the same point over and over, elaborated in almost exactly the same ways, but she wants them all typed up, redundant or no. The main point of these notes is that she is not talking about "the void," and that holes are not voids or *the void* or abysses. She seems to have a real bee in her bonnet about this; the tone of these notes is unusually vehement. "<u>A hole is not a FUCKING VOID</u>" she wrote across the top of this sheet of graph paper, with some violent underlining. Where the notes calm down a bit, she writes that voids are nothing, absences only, while a hole is, according to her, a presence. The whole point of the research TISH is doing, she writes, is to demonstrate, explore, and begin to understand what the presence of the hole means. A hole is not just missing material, she says. Everything that exists comes out of holes, that's point A. We've got that. But then we have another idea, which is that nothing comes from nothing. So, logically, the hole can't be nothing, if everything comes out of it, and nothing comes from nothing.

It's hard, writing them up, not to want to add my own unqualified remarks. What if, for example, everything that exists already exists before it comes through a hole, and the hole is only a point of admittance?

Dr. Shitansky wants holes to be things, rather than the absence of things, but at the same time she kind of categorizes them as un-things. That is, holes are things that are present as active processes engaged in de-thing-izing themselves, which is in turn what gives rise to everything else that exists, so that everything else that exists exists because of holes unmaking themselves as existing things that exist insofar and only as they actively de-exist themselves. She says that the void is just a kind of intimidation. "NO VOID" this sheet says. And then, "a hole is no void" beneath it in much smaller writing. The hole is positive, she says, and goes on to say that it not only is not negative, it is what she calls "a point of expression for being per se." I think she's trying not to present holes as magical apertures opening onto a godly plane of cosmic imaginative origination, but without saying no to the idea that it has creative properties of its own. These properties are connected to time, she says, but I can't make out how.

I also have to transcribe another video lecture by Dr. Shitansky, given around the time her book came out. At the end, the room bursts out into applause, and even cheering. Dr. Shitansky just stares. She looks nonplussed. I can't put a name to the expression on her face. I think she's stunned.

I imagine her in her homeless time, on the bus, on a park bench, on the subway, on the curb. People hurry by, look through her, shut out her voice like a bad smell. Now they cheer, they clap, the same people maybe, fuck them. Where were they back then? But this is respect, acceptance, even enthusiasm, everything the lack of which used to lacerate you like the lash of a whip—so that's it, you resent their power over you. You know it isn't gone, that power. They could all turn on me—I mean you, her—hiss and boo, and there's the street waiting, right where it always was. In an instant, you flash from the realization of a hope you were too afraid to admit you had to a second rejection ten times more final than the first. So they can cheer you and clap for you, but they can't make you believe that any of this is really yours, or that they wouldn't step over you again if you ended up back on the street. Thanks, though, really.

Was this what you dreamed about?

The throbbing in my leg and foot won't let me read. I want to read a slow, neutral, long book where nothing happens in a straightforward succession of impressionistic scenes, so I can dump out my attention on a nice even surface and let it spread, thicken in all directions, with nothing abrupt, no jolts, no highs or lows, nothing but intensely numb interest. No books here, though. It wouldn't matter if there were. All I can do is lie here. I can't even manage to sit in a chair. I can't rest my foot on the ground, and when I prop it up, the back of my leg is as tight and unyielding as a steel cable, so that leaning forward from the waist points my toes.

Look around. There's no mystery. Looking at the dark. Nothing to see, nothing to hear. Nothing there.

Pain and nothing at once and that's all. I shouldn't have to be on a path but nothing allows me to sit here and suffer. Two paths, cruel like any good choice should be: I can deny suffering or I can capitulate to it. Both paths lead to "it can't hurt me anymore." Oh, it'll still hurt, but not really, not seriously. It won't be able to damage me…or not permanently…not seriously.

Ha ha. Nothing I can decide will affect the pain itself, but I can have some fun wracking my brains trying to figure out how to feel about it and tell myself stories about what path I'm on, all the great lessons I'm learning. What did I learn from them? That there are moments when all you can do is listen in silence to what they tell you. When you really see into someone else, you don't say wow I feel that way too let's talk about it for nine hours, no, you're stunned into a silence that is more meaningful and intimate a connection that any conversation, you've been catapulted further than any mere conversation could take you.

Listening out into space. The night is so dark, I wonder if there's an outage. My eyes miss even the lines and patches of faint luminescence that usually manage to escape the blinds. I'm tempted to pull my arms out from under the covers and try feeling my eyes with my fingers, to see if they're closed, although they don't feel closed. I can feel myself blink, but I can't be sure if the blink ends with my eyes open or shut, and in the meantime there's no difference in what I see. Black, black, black, lids up or lids down. So I send my listening out into time, to hear what I can hear…

A little whoosh or a whisper, from somewhere down below, and that dull metallic thudding. It wavers up and down in volume, dwindling to nothing, then sluggishly clambering back up above the sonic threshold, if only barely. My ears ring all the time, so whatever I hear comes to me through a comb of pure, high pitches, and there's a middling one that pushes the other notes aside sometimes and seems to capture and twang them. The sound of my own ears. Beyond that, the silence sounds like mist brushing over rough stone or ceramic. It isn't the absence of all sound. There must be an absence of all sound, but I can't hear it because my hearing alone will make some noise, even without the tinnitus; there's always the unfolding boom and rustle of my nervous system.

A steady, impassive roar that starts with a remote trickle and then sweeps into a timbreless gush that seems to fill space, growing from the distance—that's what? A garbage truck? The sound dies down. I may hear or may only imagine the grating of its machinery. The sound resumes again, much fainter, and absconds back into the silence. I can situate myself in the center of a lightless pool of sound that extends for blocks and blocks in every direction, not impeded by the walls around me, if there are still any, but dammed by some of the larger buildings that I guess must be out there. Nothing happening, not even a late commuter hurrying home. Now there's the whooshing slash of a car rushing by, not far off. Imagine a short shriek of tires and a smart clap as it skids into a parked truck, the horn brays without stopping, someone's slumped over the wheel. Then there would be sirens yipping like coyotes in distant streets, the drone rises and falls over miles and miles of vacant intersections, boring through the quiet with a voice that evenly mixes apathy with anxiety while the victims lie dying, the fire burns, whatever could be rescued perishes, the victims burn...Years later, that ambulance is still on its way.

Another truck comes and goes, and out of the diminishing noise it makes, footsteps in the street. Each step is distinct, an echo follows them. The sound conjures an imaginary film with glistening asphalt and the lone silhouette of the one out there, carrying on its back like wings the burgeoning pennants of a jewelled and petalled world it brings, only in order to deny me all its fiery pellucid colors and pure timbres. I'm not allowed not to know the place that banishes me, so the one out there is on their way to make the confirmation. The steps recede and approach, grow louder, grow softer, but they're always under-lined and clear.

It calls on the pain, and the pain responds, worsening the closer it gets to me, then flaring up even worse when it strays off track. The pain only ebbs in order to surge, so, when it draws near again, the pain leaps up to encourage it. The one out there homes in. They want to get through, to *get in*, and try to come in here with me.

They will sit down by my bed and touch my arm, like they're comforting me, but, under a gentle hand and mockery of compassion, their magic opens the infinity in the pain. They're here to show me my one endlessness is my capacity for more pain. No limits there. Above an expression of tender care, the musical weather of heaven resounds on the other side of the ceiling and the complete absence of light, absence of peace, the other side, the black brane.

Dr. Corngholm, the linguist, never settled in any particular office, he just slips and slides. He drinks water on a schedule, according to Ph and time of day. Wherever he is, he has two or three plain water bottles in front of him, on his desk, on a shelf, labelled, by him, with their Ph number. There's a picture of him, too, that he always sets up somewhere, showing him in a jungle setting surrounded by men in loin cloths—the Amazon? A portrait of himself, too, in pencil, signed "Guillaume," will always turn up on a nearby wall.

Getting him his mail was a chore at first, until we worked out an arrangement whereby I leave his mail in a basket on top of the toilet tank in his favorite bathroom stall. Of course he has a favorite bathroom stall. He's never around, but, when I check the basket again at the end of my mail route, his mail is always gone. I don't follow a strict schedule myself, so I guess he must be watching for me in the shadows somewhere. He and Allegre are friendly and from time to time I skirt the fringe of one of their spectral conversations.

Dr. Liu is maybe a little younger than fifty. On her desk, a photo of her with her very serious husband smiling his tight-lipped smile. Here she is getting an award. Here she is with her two kids. Here she is singing in a chorus. In all the family photos on her bookshelves it looks as though they were being bombarded with light as part of a physics experiment. Each picture is all but washed out in flash blaze that seems to radiate into the room, making each frame a little panel of light among the books. Her desk is more spartan, a bit like Dr. Shitansky's. Whenever I swing by, she's always working out some calculations on a tablet of graph paper, stabbing numbers into an archaic Burroughs calculating machine and consulting a slide rule she keeps in a special little leather case. Her father and mother were both engineers and they taught her mathematics using an old bakelite Victor Champion and their own slide rules, which makes her a natural fit for TISH.

"I don't think many physicists would have the patience to work like this!" she says.

She makes coffee with sweetened condensed milk in it, and she always brews extra in case anyone drops by for a chat. As far as I know, I'm the only one here who does. Renbrui comes by now and then, but only to give orders. Dr. Liu likes me because I ask her about string theory; she takes pleasure in explaining complicated things to clowns like me. She says that her study of black branes is the main point of contact between her research and Dr. Shitansky's.

"String theory generally suggests that we can resolve the problems of conventional physics by postulating the existence of seven additional dimensions beyond the three we know plus the one additional dimension of time. About ten or eleven in total. These additional dimensions are hard to detect because they're very small, riddling the vaster dimensions we know. There may even be whole other universes tucked away in dimensional micro-apertures surrounding and permeating us right now. The problem is that there is no clear way to demonstrate any of this. It only makes sense mathematically—the only strong point in the theory's favor is that it weathers the mathematic challenge. Studying an extreme object, like a black hole, or black brane, could yield more tangible evidence for or against the theory."

Daladara doesn't hang around. If you see him, he's doing something or he's leaving. All business. I thought at first maybe that he doesn't like white people; then I found out he was born in Sweden. So now I don't know. He's never hostile to me, nor to anyone at TISH. He sits by the decoherence reactor for long stretches of time, snapping his abacus with a look of strained concentration on his face, with now and then a pause to jot notes in a little notebook. Or he sits outside at one of the picnic tables in the shade of the old locust tree with nonstop tea and cigarettes, doing cut-ups with the newspaper, entering the data on his abacus. He told me he made it himself out of iroko wood, with pearl-like white porcelain beads.

Remembering now, I'm not sure why, back when desire was so fierce wild and uncoupled from anything real it was just madness, when the blink of a certain eye was like a blow to the head and I'd stagger through a delirious day, head home reeling in a dream that even the end of the world couldn't stop.

How much have I got back there composting in past time, fuming, turning into something else that still insists it's mine, even though I'm already gone?

An old man's question.

—Which is to say, a rhetorical one.

My own ghost shot back into me from out of heaven, terrifying, afraid of me—it doesn't want to go back to being me again, me again, again me, me: me, that's the last thing I want, last thing someone wants...heaven is beautiful pain, irresistably alluring terror, out of the music, the not-me there, irradiated with ugly compassion I was never coming back—

    me again
    not me again
    I don't want it
    someone doesn't

to be perfected in pain and pleasure alike you can't have mastery over the word...it's painpleasure...pleasain...painsure...

languid play of sunbeams
each is a timeless scream of anguish, terror, and loss
the beautiful grieflight
whose beams trail like fronds
shedding dignity down on the suffusiongrounds

the lastingness...
Ernie Allegre is the engineer—

One more time—
Ernie Allegre is the engineer.
"They take it for granted," Allegre says around a mouthful of cake.
"Everything has to be simple.
"It's a prejudice of science."
He swallows his mouthful.
"So they do experiments, and the experiments validate the simple ideas.
"But what if everything just looks simple the way they do it?
"What if the simplicity is only a function of the way they measure things?
"In some ways I guess it makes sense that the simplest answer is the most likely natural answer, but isn't it just as logical to think that the bigger something is, the more complicated it is?
"I mean, you take a building, big building, with a very simple, boxy design.
"You still have, like, an oil stain on the third floor that's seeping into the concrete at a rate of so many bits of a millimeter a month, and there's metal parts that are more exposed in one spot so they oxidize faster just there, and there's places where

there's more strain and cracks and places where there's less, all kinds of structural irregularities that add up to some pretty significant things—and then, there's a really complicated design for a building that, when you build it, it turns out the design takes all these factors of stress, weathering and wear and tear into account so the building stays steady state.

"So you can have simplicity inside complexity, no problem.

"The universe is on such a grand scale.

"It makes sense it would be really complicated, and there'd be all kinds of variations and irregularities.

"No one knows the overall shape, and they want to say it's shaped this way or that, simple geometric shapes, but who even knows what the limits of the universe look like?

"No one's seen them.

"You could be looking right at them and you wouldn't know.

"They could be all around us right now.

"If it's a void, then that's nothing, so you could be seeing the end of the universe right now and you'd be seeing nothing, just what's around you, like the end of the universe is overlaid on everything right here, right now, and you see it all the time, but you don't know it.

"Why would you?

"So fuck it.

"Right?

"You don't know."

And Daladara says: "See, what happened was, the world itself was fundamentally changed when someone came up with a number for nothing. You know that nothing was just a joke, right? It kept going as a joke, too, and like a lot of jokes it turned on its joker; because zero is a hole and holes, aren't nothing after all, just like Dr. Shitansky says. Adding, subtracting, and dividing by zero don't do anything, but multiplying by zero turns anything into zero, and that means, 'we're waiting.' There's some of this quantity around, just not here, so we can't say how many there are. But if you say three times zero equals zero, that just means there's no threes. There could be twos, or ones, or fours, or thousands, but just no threes. And besides, there is still a number there, called zero. You can't not have a number, any more than a hole can be nothing."

"I would have thought negative numbers were the holes of the number world," I say lamely.

"No that's just which side of the teeter-totter you're on. Negative means you're missing this many, but the 'slots' for those things are still there and there's this many 'slots.' Zero, though, that's the number that every actual number comes out of, in base ten or base two or whatever."

He takes a long pull on his cigarette, releasing the smoke in a jet from each nostril. Another quick pull and a sharp inhalation to chase it down after, then out again. Look around, mourning dove calls, car whooshes by.

"Once something has fulfilled its purpose," he says, "the magic that sustains it ends. You have to become an unperson to keep the magic going."

"Like a human zero?"

"Yup," he says, and takes another drag.

Leaning forward, elbows on knees, necktie dangles, squint, scan the world.

"I don't know how it works for other people. But for me, the hybridizing brings in the power of its distance. The tension of holding the disparate elements together is creative."

"Going to the coordinates" is something that Daladara has to do, and since he doesn't drive, that leaves it to me to drive him there. His abacus tells him the latitude and longitude and then he has to map them laboriously with a paper map and draw lines with rulers and so on. Then he has to go there and do his thing.

"I'm sorry man, I'm going to have to smoke in your car," he says.

"Well we're driving with the windows down, then."

"I prefer it," he says.

I wasn't introduced to Daladara in any particular moment, but over a period of time. He's a spare, straight-backed, deliberate man of fixed habits who always seems to look exactly the same, making whatever he wears or does sort of emblematic of him. He wears a plain black suit and kind of a dark maroon tie, brown dress shoes, carries a briefcase where he keeps his abacus and notebook and gear and a thermos of tea. Orange foam headphones full of Albert Ayler and Steve Reich, his fibrous hands carefully extracting the cassettes from their cases and easing them precisely into his portable tape player, a pen and a pencil side by side in his breast pocket. A dark, bright, haggard face with five o'clock shadow and darting, nervous eyes that tag and interrelate everything they see. He has a way of making sure he's always out of place wherever he is; I have the idea that he's only at ease out of place, like he wants an open antagonism with time and place so he can keep his eye on them. Then again, he has a way of seeming jittery, or sometimes even wobbly, but being completely stable when you actually check on him.

He drops into the seat beside me and lights up.

"I thought white lighters were bad luck," I say.

"Not for the guy who sells them," he says. "You want to buy it?"

He puts on his headphones and jabs repeatedly at the power button on his tape player as I pull out into traffic.

"Any problem if I turn my radio on?"

"No," he shakes his head without looking up from his misbehaving power button. "I prefer it."

He snaps the button again and flips his middle finger at it. The tape starts playing.

"The cross-talk between tracks adds another layer," he says, dribbling ash down his lapel. He scoops it up with a deft waft of his hand and releases it out the open window.

Once we get onto the highway and start zooming through the hills, he opens his briefcase, takes out a graph paper tablet, corners pinned down with paperclips against the wind, and starts sketching. He'll look up, his eyes will seize something we happen to be flashing past, and he'll enter it into the composite landscape he's building. It's a real landscape, not an imaginary one—everything he draws is real, something he had in front of him I mean, somehow, but it's not a landscape you could see for yourself unless you reproduced this ride, these glimpses. The result is an insidiously banal-looking drawing that doesn't announce the way it was made.

"What happens when we get there?" I ask.

"I have to change something there. I'll see it when I know it."

He rocks side to side, holding the top of the door between his fingers, eyes scanning the landscape.

"Is this for your TISH thing?"

"Yeah," he nods. His gaze is like a shoal or a flock that gets disrupted when I ask questions and then reforms.

"And you do...?"

I almost said "mathematical magic," which sounds too corny, like "mathemagic." I don't want any stern looks.

"...you calculate something?"

"No," he says. "It's description. It's not calculation. I use my abacus the same way you use a musical instrument. As I describe, I check the numbers that come out. But I don't calculate with them. Every number has a plan associated with it. As the numbers change during the description, the plans get to interact."

"And that's showing you...what's that showing you?"

The question amuses him. On second thought, I think it's my curiosity that amuses him.

"It doesn't *show* me anything," he says.

He has his cigarette between his fingers, not dangling from his lips, which means he's inclined to talk.

"It's what I'm making that I see. I mean, when you say something—are you *showing* yourself anything when you say something?"

"I may give myself away."

"Sure, but do you talk in order to make yourself do that?"

"Well, no."

"Well, no," he says, with a trace of mimicry. "Me, I'm *making* something, not *showing* something."

"I guess you threw me off when you said you were describing things."

"How did I throw you off?"

"You said you were describing something and now you say you're making something. Making and describing aren't the same thing."

"You make a description, don't you?"

"Yeah, but that isn't the thing."

"Yeah, but that is *a* thing, right? The description is *a* thing. You can have one mountain and a thousand descriptions. As many descriptions as there are people seeing it. Even the same person sees it differently at different times."

"But the description is only useful because it relates back to what it describes, though."

"OK, but it has to be something else if it's going to relate *back*. Turn off here."

We pull into a drugstore parking lot. Daladara flicks his cigarette onto the ground and opens the car door.

"You stay here. I have to go do a thing," he says. "Listen, when I come out—don't talk to me until I talk to you, OK?"

I nod. "OK."

"And don't touch me, either. I don't guess you'd be likely to, but just in case."

"Sure, fine...Say, how long is this going to be?"

"Don't know. But I won't linger."

He gets out of the car and walks swiftly over to the drugstore entrance, his whole body loose in his suit jacket and slacks. A woman stops about ten feet away from the car on the other side and turns—

"Rose! You need mustard?"

An indistinct reply from somewhere behind me.

"What's that? Oh, OK."

She makes her way into the drugstore. I get out of the car, stretch, ramble a little up and down, looking at the blue with two unrelated feathery tufts of cloud in two completely different parts of the sky, wonder if everything really does happen for a reason, study the continent-sized sky in alternation with the pebbly, friable blacktop, the congealed white paint bunched up on top of it. Turn around and my crummy little car looks convex and even smaller than usual: a trusty moon buggy. Sit down inside, and everything is normal.

Daladara is coming back, lighting a cigarette, squinting. He opens the car door, pulls out his briefcase, sets it on the roof, and for a while his torso and legs are framed in the doorway. Overhead I can hear the click of his abacus and the scratching of his pencil on a sheet of paper. Then I hear him toss everything into the briefcase, snap its two latches shut. He sets it down upright in the footwell and gets in around it, shutting the door, nods to me.

"All set."

Since the dramatics of the scene are calling for it, I start the motor and pull out.

"What did you do in there?"

"I can't tell you."

"Why not?"

"What do you mean, 'why not?'"

"I already know you're doing magic."

"Yeah, but then you should know magic is all about keeping secrets. Secrets are power, you know that."

"I haven't told you what I had for breakfast this morning. That's not giving me any power that I've noticed."

"Asking questions is also about power," he says.

I feel rebuked and don't say anything.

"You make your secrets," he says after a moment. "And you make them the kind of secret that does something for you. So your not telling me what you had for breakfast—by itself that's neither here nor there. But there's no reason you can't make it a secret that does something for you. If you tell me what you had for breakfast today, and I can use that to pin a murder on you somehow, then that secret matters, suddenly."

"Is that what Shitansky thinks?"

"Probably not. She's interested in control. She needs to know where all the pieces are and that none of them are going astray. I mean, who's going to try to steal a bunch of bullshit about holes? I don't mean it is bullshit, but that's how it has to look from outside, and Shitansky prefers it like that. She doesn't care whether people think she's nuts or not."

We ride along a little, and then he speaks again.

"Her work is her own thing playing off of all our things, mine, Allegre's, Corngholm's...She has her thing and she monitors what everyone else is doing, and relates it all together in her mind. Then she processes it some way and the picture that she sees is telling her something about holes. She runs it all through the hole in her brain and then checks the results."

I don't get premonitions, but I might have had one a night or two before Dr. Shitansky announced her own experiment. After what had seemed like a long day, with running to and fro, I'd left TISH and was heading for the parking lot when I suddenly sat down on one of the benches there. I don't know why I did it. My motives were all negative. I didn't want to be in the building any more, and I didn't want to drive, and I didn't want to wander. I didn't want to sit, either, but I did.

I breathed in the blue air of late dusk turning into dark, feeling the mountains behind me like an obscure fire pouring blue down on us below. The brutalist hives were on my left, TISH was right in front of me, dim gold visible through a stand of eucalyptus trees. After some minutes had passed, my senses numbly registered that a light was on in TISH. I could see only the one light, in one room, through the floor-to-ceiling window. As I continued to pay attention to this light, which wasn't bright, I gradually learned that it was a pale yellow light shining down from a desk lamp onto a desk, where Dr. Shitansky was sitting. I didn't think that was her office, but I could have been turned around, or she could have been sitting in some other office, since she had the run of the place. She was sitting there with both her hands on the desk in front of her, head thrust forward heavily, not moving, but even from this distance I could somehow see that her eyes were blinking, not closed. Bas was sitting upright beside her on the floor. It was as if they were both transfixed by something on the far side of the room.

I had no will to look away. I had a feeble impulse casting around for some performable action, like "going home," or "not spying," but it couldn't manage to latch on to anything, and so I stayed where I was like a rag doll tossed in a corner. My gaze grew heavy. Dr. Shitansky wasn't doing anything; she sat motionless and impassive as an Egyptian statue. My mind went to sleep, while my eyes watched. There was a sound like something whisking a piece of plastic fabric; I guess it was a bird. A night bird. They usually don't have pretty cries. The blue blackened around the window and the light swam inside its own outlines. I had a momentarily disembodied feeling, to be drawn out and physically sustained in the dusk and the isolation of the one light.

Something important was happening. It was a forgetting. I was drawn into it. Not as a witness. I joined with it. I melted in still shadow. Time pooled in my shape; it welled up inside me. I knew I could leave it and rejoin the usual succession of events at any moment, just by standing up, or even by shifting my body slightly. My position, the placement of my head, the curve in my spine, the slackness in my arms, the pressure of my feet against the ground, which Dr. Liu says is all a matter of electromagnetic fields, are all at least potentially necessary to this event. Alteration of any of them will break the spell, if only for me—and that's bound to happen, unless this comes to an end before I move.

Dr. Shitansky is turning into a Cezanne painting. None of the details of her appearance are lost on me, but they combine into an abstract image, like what an alien would see, looking at a human being. You'd think she'd be the alien here, not me, with the hole in her brain, like the unaccountable trace of an abduction by a UFO. Maybe she's turning into an alien. So is Bas, though. All of her details are clear, but they fit together like a collage. Everything I see wavers back and forth between being abstract and looking like they always do, and yet, there really is no visible difference from one to the other, only a difference in vision. It's like I'm seeing a variation in vision that has nothing personally to do with me, or with her.

"She's listening to what's coming through the hole in her brain," I thought.

I don't remember how it ended. I got up. I must have. And then I went home. I must have. For all I know I went to a bar and shot a man but I think I went straight home, and the next day, or maybe the day after that, Dr. Shitansky called us together and announced her big project.

That forgetting never left me, by the way. It rides around with me like an invisible halo. A hole of light for my head to rest in.

Dr. Shitansky's idea is to cut a hole in a substance that can be precisely worked, even when thin.

"The material has to be at maximum thinness to express a hole with minimum impurities," she says, and then turns to Allegre.

"What's the best material for that?"

He shrugs.

"Depends on how big a hole you want, what you do with it..."

"I'm going to put my head in it and listen," Dr. Shitansky says, raising her hands up by her ears. "It has to be suspended with minimum contact to anything else, and lowered down so my head is in the hole. I have to be able to sit down while I have the hole around my head, so I can listen for as long as my mental endurance lasts."

"You could do that with anything. Plastic, sheet metal, glass, ceramic, wood..."

Dr. Shitansky drops her hands to the desk top in front of her and spreads them out.

"OK, the neutrality of the material should be maximum," she says. "It shouldn't have been alive at any time. I can try listening to a hole in a leaf if there are leaves that big...there must be leaves big enough for that. Do leaves come that big, Renbrui?"

"How should I know?" Renbrui says flatly. "You want me to look up big leaves?"

"Look them up!" Dr. Shitansky says, slamming the flat of

her hand on the desk with a report that shivers against the walls. "I want to know my options!"

Renbrui primly jots "BIG LEAF" on her clipboard.

"We'll start with metal," Dr. Shitansky says.

She holds out her hands, palms down, pressed edgewise together, forming a sheet.

"The metal has to be stiff enough so that there's no sagging at all, minimum, *I mean minimum* sag, so the hole is not distorted. It has to be flat—flat—and at maximum thinness."

"Minimum thickness," Allegre says.

"Exactly," Dr. Shitansky says. "Now what kind of metal will not give when it's thin?"

"Again it depends on how thin, on the dimensions."

"I said minimum thickness."

"Right, but how big is the thing you're talking about?"

Dr. Shitansky holds her hands up like bookends, about four inches out from the sides of her head. Allegre gets up, pulling a tape measure from his coverall, and draws out a length of tape across the distance, standing behind Dr. Shitansky.

"Twenty-eight inches even, across," he says. "Now how deep?"

"Which way is that? Side to side? Back to front?"

"Yup."

"Back to front?"

"Yup."

"Then say it!"

"Back to front!"

Dr. Shitansky sits with her hands on the desk. A moment passes when we all just look at each other.

"What's the size back to front?" Allegre asks.

Dr. Shitansky's hands move: one in front of her face, the other behind her head, with her elbow craned around. Allegre steps to one side of her and measures.

"Seventeen and a quarter," he says.

Dr. Shitansky waits for Allegre to sit down again. Bas is still lying with her chin on the floor. I should try that myself sometime; I think the posture would suit me.

"What's the best material for maximum thinness without bending at all at twenty-eight inches even across, seventeen and a quarter inches back to front?"

"Aluminum," he says.

"OK, make me a sheet of aluminum that size. It should have holes in the corners for anchoring wires to."

"How wide a hole do you want?"

Again her hands go up, and Allegre measures.

"Twelve and three quarters inches."

"I just had my hair cut," she says. "We'll start with an even thirteen."

"Any specifications about the thickness?"

"Whatever is the thinnest it can be without any sagging," Dr. Shitansky says, getting suddenly to her feet. She pulls a big pad of poster-sized drawing paper from a side drawer and holds it up, showing us a pretty good pencil sketch done by her. It shows a figure, roughly herself, seated in a chair surrounded by ranks of what look like identical topiaries, both serried and staggered in a kind of labyrinth, which are labelled "acoustic panels." A flat sheet, not quite parallel to the ground, hangs suspended from wires in each corner, dangling from four little motorized winches anchored at the upper corners of a cubical frame around the chair. Arrows indicate that the sheet can be raised or lowered, and that its attitude can also be changed, rotating it forward or backward or to one or the other side, even upright. The figure in the chair sits with her hands on the arms and her head through the hole, so that her eyes and most of her nose protrude above the sheet. An arrow leads from the word "LISTENING" to the figure's head.

"We'll use the auditorium space," she says. "The acoustic panels will have to be arranged so that there's an island of maximum silence in the center, and then we'll put the chair in the silence and we can listen to hear if anything comes out of the hole we've made in the minimum-thickness-material. I'll report orally on whatever I hear and Renbrui will take dictation. Then we can have Gross type it up for the record. I'll need a thermometer, a barometer, a slide rule, a crystal radio set, and some kind of minimally electronic audio recording equipment. These can be stored in the control booth here."

She points to a crudely-drawn box with a large panel in front of it, facing the chair, and labelled "two-way glass" with an arrow.

"Allegre, I want you to look at the lighting in the auditorium and set it up for maximum frequency uniformity, so we can have a neutral light background in case there are any light changes."

I had gone to the beach, by myself. There was an anniversary I wanted to remember there. The day was overcast, the beach was mostly deserted, which suited me. I walked in the sand, wearing myself out, going first up the shore and then down again, until I was too tired to feel anything anymore. As I made my way back to the parking lot, the wind lowered, the waves became almost silent, and the mist began turning into light rain.

Stepping from the sand to the crumbling asphalt pathway, I felt a little like a compressed spring that had finally come loose, and then, in the same moment, I caught sight of Dr. Shitansky's car, tucked away in a corner by a clump of agave plants and low palms in the far corner of the lot. It might not have been hers, but that make, that new, that color, you didn't see that often. I came to this beach in particular because it was the easiest to reach from my place; so, maybe Shitansky found it convenient too? She didn't strike me as the beachgoing type, but why not? I could imagine her in grey sweats doing push ups, jogging stolidly on the sand.

Should I bother her? There was a pathway there, leading from the lot's edge back into the dunes. I followed it, hoping to catch sight of her without being seen myself. There was only just enough desire in me to justify the effort of spying on her. Fraternizing with her was beyond me; come to think of it, it would always be beyond me.

The path curled around the palms into a little concreted area with picnic tables and grill racks. No sign of anyone. Then, I noticed someone sitting on one of the benches, engulfed in a white hoodie. She had a long skirt, and was sitting with her legs crossed, head down, a cigarette between two long straight fingers. The mist suddenly congealed into drops, heavy ones. She started up and rushed, holding herself in her arms, hustling toward the lot along the cement walkway that vanished on the far side of the palms from me. I heard the solid tread of her boots stop, and moment later the slam of a car door.

I backtracked a little, until I could see the lot again. The car I had taken for Dr. Shitansky's was weaving toward the exit. I saw white-shrouded arms switch and wave as the driver worked the steering wheel. The hood slipped from her head, and I saw flyaway locks, long and curly. The car pulled out into traffic. I walked over to the bench where she had been sitting, took in the little heap of cigarette butts marked with red lipstick, the four little empty whiskies.

Maybe she has an anniversary to commemorate, too, I thought. When I saw her the next day at work, she was the same as usual. I studied her as closely as I dared, and I know she caught me staring at least once because I saw a look of irritation —I mean, *greater* irritation—flash across her face just then. Otherwise, I couldn't really imagine, let alone see, any connection between this erect, efficient, brisk, businesslike woman and the miserable, dejected figure, all but slumped on a park bench, that had flashed by me the day before. That didn't matter, though, because I knew they were the same.

I know you're alone, Renbrui. There's being alone for the moment, and then there's another kind of solitude, which is essential. That's the way I'm alone, that's the way the woman on the beach was alone, and that's the isolation I see in you every day, Renbrui. It's what we have in common.

Dr. Liu explained her experiment to me, drawing down the blinds and firing up her overhead projector. The slides didn't do much to enhance my understanding.

"I study a phenomenon called quantum entanglement. All particles have a property that we call 'spin.'"

She flares her eyes when she says "spin," her enthusiastic smile is almost a grimace.

"It has nothing to do with spinning, though. It's just a term we use to discuss a certain state the particle is in. When two particles are entangled, that means that when you determine the spin of one, you also determine the spin of the other one, no matter how far apart they are. All particles have spin, but the funny thing about it is...is that it is only determined when measured, when you measure it. When we measure spin, we determine it. So a spin that hasn't been measured is, you know, there, but it isn't determined up or down. It has no direction.

"I should say, there's two types of spin—spin up, and spin down. Until we measure it, all the particle has is just spin: no up, no down, just undetermined spin. Only when we measure it does the particle have spin up or spin down. That's true of any particle.

"But, when you have *entangled* particles, then, when the one particle is measured, and its spin is determined, the other particle's spin will also be determined, and—and this is the main thing, the weird thing—at exactly the same moment—in reverse!"

She speaks these last words with great emphasis, underlining how outrageous they are. Shadow of her ballpoint on the overhead slide, indicating two vibrating points thrown up on the wall.

"So, if I measure particle A and determine it has spin up, then particle B will be determined with spin down in the same moment. This happens immediately, no matter how far apart the two particles are, and that caused Einstein a big headache because that meant that something had been found that goes faster than light."

She grins at me and gives a little snort, wrinkling her nose. You can tell when she's hit on something that she thinks is especially interesting, because she has a way of rearing against the back of her chair and slightly exaggerating her enunciation when she mentions it.

"My experiment involves trying to use quantum entanglement to better understand black holes, or black branes. If the experiment works, it might help us to decide, among other things, whether what we're looking at is a black hole or black brane, since the experiment offers the opportunity possibly to prove some of the underpinning premises of string theory. What I'm trying to get done is that we get hold of some particles that are entangled with particles that are falling into a black hole or brane."

Here she crooks her hand in the air, like she were physically taking hold of the particles.

"These structures are surrounded with what is called an event horizon, which is the point of no return for anything falling into them. Basically, once an object has passed the event horizon, it's impossible for us to make any further observations about it under normal conditions. It might have vanished from the universe altogether, or it might be in there somehow..."

She waggled her head and waved her hands to indicate the mysteriousness of the idea of something being "in there somehow."

"But if we can find some entangled particles about to fall into a black hole, and we can find the particles that they're entangled with somewhere else, where they are *not* falling into a black hole, or black brane, then we *can* observe what is happening inside the black hole or brane, at least as far as spin is concerned."

And now, as she speaks, her face is suffused with a quiet, limpid sort of joy. Something especially pure. She brandishes her index finger.

"If we measure the spin of a particle outside the event horizon, then we would determine the spin within the event horizon at the same time. However, it's possible the extreme distortion of time and space in there could cause spin to act strangely. There are *all sorts* of possibilities. If there are spin anomalies, or even spin warping, then this might make it possible for us to get some evidence of the existence of multiple other dimensions beyond the familiar ones we already know exist, which could constitute new experimental or observational evidence for the validity of string theory."

She drops her hands into her lap and smiles at me, raising her eyebrows as if to say, well, how about that!

"The tricky part will be in locating the particles and detecting the entanglement."

My left foot is bad today. I was able to drive to TISH anyway and hobble to my desk. As long as I can get something done here, you know. My existence gets through another day without being unjustified. Daladara comes by to keep me company, bringing a chair with him and offering me a box of orange juice. He tells me about his morning. On a bench at a stop for a bus he wasn't going to take, he looks across the street and sees a woman waiting for her husband or whatever to bring the car around and zoom her away, and he says she plucked a thread out of the air with a single, assured gesture, then pocketed it.

"A paranoid's problem is that he understands everything that goes on around him too well," he says. "You've got to keep things Zaman Wislin."

I don't know what those two words mean, but he throws them around as if I did, and I, so far, have never chosen to ask him. The more often he says them, and the more often I let them go by, the more embarrassing that question becomes.

"It's important to leave things sketchy in your mind if you want to see more," he says.

"No problem."

"The plan is there; the world is a hole that leaks correspondences. The question for me is whether you can see the world itself, or only just this or that expression. Is it in its nature to be perceived as itself? The world, not just the planet but everything, so the cosmos. The stars do affect us, just not the way the astrologers say."

I don't know and I don't care. He's telling me about being affected by stars now? Are we doing this?

Am I going to keep on breaking down like this? How long is this string going to be, and how long before the next string breaks, when a moment's reflection makes it all into a failure beyond question? I catch a sharp smell of artificial lemon, look down and see a triangle on the earth. I miss the open horizon, the weird powdery blue of the ribbon blurring the darkening landscape, a pale yellow in high mist, the suede brown soil, the chill coming across the porthole as the sun washes out of thunderheads like chess pieces. Blue blue blue boiling away behind me. And me, in transit, nobody in particular and no need to be anyone just then. Between selves.

Come in for a landing. So then, what's left? Sad people with their sad choices, seen sadly. So is all this false? Compared to what? This street scene with coffee ice cream or the empyrean on the painbed in my little room? What I *can* tell you is that none of it is good.

Listening unfolds like a limitless sail that billows out into an obscurity, maybe day, night, or something else. A mourning dove's voice interrupts the sound. My hearing responds, alien spirits answer in mangled human accents, with syllables that skip and dance across the peaks of the noise, a ponderous carolling that's driven by the exhausting pain in my legs. It clangs, tolls, booms. A dull metallic thudding, a mute appeal to the sky for mercy, to plunge into frigid blue and white, that furnace of ice and gale winds whose invisible violence is suspended so high above the ground, transfixed in radiation and a trembling skein of razor-sharp cold and insane speed. That's heaven. Faster and faster. You can't outrun death, but at high speed you can spread your death out over a lot of room. And that means, over a lot of time.

Figures stand perfectly still on rigidly soft cloud peaks, like contemplative, vigilant columns, gaze down dark slopes with blazing outlines. They're aware of me, but they pay me no mind. I'm part of the scene. Froth skates past me and scatters its threads, melts in the cold sky-furnace, but where's the sun? It's always behind me. I can't see myself, either, but I can just about feel the radiation pour past me, rush everywhere, eternally at its business, at travel, while, in the depths of the sky, I know there's a black brane. A string connects it to me. Behind the blue, it's dreaming there, the end. I'm panting heavily, but that's because of the pain. Death behind the sky, with its string in me, reel me on in without any haste. This pain won't kill me. It's just a friendly reminder that the body is destructible. It has that power, to be destroyed.

"All about messages," Daladara goes on. "OK, messages from where? Everybody asks that—"

"I didn't."

"—but that's where you go lose it. You stay with the message. It's not like the message isn't from anywhere, but the from-ness is the message. The from-ness is the message. That there is a from to *from* from now that there's a message."

"You mean it makes the place it's from?"

"Kind of," he says, "but not sort of."

"The message comes first, then the source?"

"No, neither of them comes first. They happen to each other all together. But the message—what makes the message a message is that you can notice it, while you can't notice where it's from. You have to get the message first to know the from-ness is there. Without the message you don't ever know that it's there, but when you do know it's there, you realize it's...not familiar, but...familiarly alien, a familiar alien."

Daladara often talks as though he's on the verge of giving up the attempt at a description.

"An alien familiar?"

"An alien familiar," he says. "That's not bad, that's Zaman Wislin."

No one is supposed to enter the auditorium without a reason, especially when Dr. Shitansky is sitting an experiment. My first reason came with an urgent message for Renbrui, a number she has to call right away—a lawyer's number. The heavy double doors swing open with a soft hiss of pneumatics. A strong gust of that clean backstage linseed oil smell. Black panels of acoustic foam ten feet tall stand between each row of seats, turning the aisle in front of me into a causeway through a high hedge maze. The path to the sunken, round stage area is staggered in shallow steps, giving me a feeling of not quite being in control of my momentum as I make my way down. With each step I take, the silence deepens around me. Just here I have to sidestep around a baffle, and from this point on my path zigzags around panels that fill even the steps. The floor levels out, and I can see the dimly-glowing spotlights in the truss overhead; that's the only clue I have to let me know I'm more or less on the stage.

Tape arrows on the floor point me through the baffles, which now seem to be arranged in punctuated circles with offset openings. A long curving stretch of unbroken space takes me nearly to the back of the hall, so that, when I do finally emerge from this noiseless, artificial forest I'm behind the control booth. This is a plywood structure covered in dull greyish-black acoustic foam, one door centered in the back with a small window.

PRESS BUTTON DON'T KNOCK the sticky note over the doorbell says.

I press the button without hearing anything, but I see a light flash inside the booth. A moment later a shadow fills the glass window in the door and it pops open a crack—there's Renbrui, standing very close. Small white teeth in crimson gums, floral fragrance.

"Yeah?"

I hand her the slip.

"This lawyer called for you," I say, realizing that I've been mentally sorting my words to get this message succinct enough for her. "She said you should call her back today before five; that it was urgent."

She has already taken the slip and is scanning it with pursed lips.

"Right," she says absently, and disappears, the door closing with a noiseless clap.

I take this opportunity to dawdle over by the corner of the booth and peep around at Dr. Shitansky. She's sitting in what must be the center of the stage, in a gleaming aluminum frame office chair, Bas lying beside it with her chin on the floor. A thin sheet of metal about two feet square hangs suspended from four wires, one anchored to each corner. The wires run back to little power winches fixed to upright struts that form an incomplete metal cube around her. The metal sheet has a hole in it big enough to admit her head, and it has been lowered down parallel to the ground, until it hangs just below the bridge of her nose.

Dr. Shitansky sits perfectly still, listens tensely, her eyes tightly shut, her hands gripping the arms of the chair, head thrust a bit forward, feet flat on the floor. It's like she's submerged up to her eyeballs in silence, just the top of her head protruding above the level of the metal sheet, which hangs without swinging, as if it were welded there in space. I can hear each long, heavy breath she takes, and another sound that might be the minute squeal of teeth grating together in her mouth.

Her breathing accelerates. Her face clenches in a continuous, steady accumulation of tension that curls the left corner of her upper lip in a mechanical sneer.

She makes a sharp, impatient gesture with her right hand, her wrist still glued to the arm of the chair. The little winches in the frame whir, lifting the sheet of metal until it hangs suspended about a foot above Dr. Shitansky's head. She lets her breath out in a gust, and Bas, her familiar, rises to a sitting position, looking at her. The tension drains from her features, and pink starts to supplant the grey in her cheeks. Her eyelids loosen. When the whirring stops, she makes to get up, freezes, listening intently, then notices me.

"Oh, it's you," she says with disappointment, and kneads her eyes with her right hand.

It isn't the first time I've heard those words directed at me, and uttered in that tone. I'm not aware of having made any noise, though.

"Sorry," I say.

She doesn't answer, but rises to her feet, keeping her head low so as not to knock it against the sheet. Once erect, she sways slightly.

"Renbrui, did you make note of that heart spike?" she calls.

The PA clicks on inside the booth.

"Two minutes fourteen seconds," Renbrui's voice says, flat in the speaker.

Dr. Shitansky shakes her head.

"Two forty-five," she says. "Log that."

"Logged."

She turns to me.

"You stay."

Then, to the booth—"Give him today's transcript now, since he's already here."

"Right."

"I want a medical examination. There was pain there, at the end. Non-minimal pain."

She presses the palm of her right hand hard against the middle of her forehead, eyes shut again.

"It was hole-related," she says.

c Judging from the outside, and from the overhead photograph, you wouldn't think this place has hallways. It's the sort of place with covered walkways and paths, or it should be, but this place is nothing but wide, sterilized halls with greenish floors dully gleaming in the paltry light that filters in from outdoors. Dingy white tile up to chest height along the walls, a kind of clinic. The empty kind. You would think, though, if you didn't know it from the inside, that this was an apartment building, not even a very big one.

Always in my ears and at my back I hear the hush and whine of ghostly short wave, peppered with fragmentary sounds, warped and drawling half-words made wry and sybilline by the distortion, enveloped in a quick echo that snatches at meaning and shivers it, without quite breaking its tension—one endless fragment of time always repeating and always different, voices call to each other in the dark, cry out, bellow in rage, panic, and pain...gloating, condescending voices like curtains of unctuous, smothering brown gauze that collapse resistance beneath their weight and capture every foreign impulse in a tacky adhesive effluvium of knowing looks, neutralizing worldliness, the wisdom of the already-there, already-finished. Space rings like a bell with their voices, forever, boring into my brain without bothering my ears.

That's my life out there—there's the darkness, and you can almost see it, like transparencies flickering by, a long shout elongated by a kind of time distortion. You can almost see it, like a powdery coil of minute, faintly luminous grains stretching itself in the deep water at the ocean bottom, in outer space. You can almost see her, the way she is now. A ghost. I say you can almost see her. Did I ever see her better than almost?

The darkness I see with my eyes closed isn't pure, though. There's a translucent, pitted film of some nameless color that fills the expanse, and very dim blue-black and violent shapes disrupt, erupt, pop and fade there without any corresponding physical sensation or apparent stimulus. They're just *there,* and then they're gone in a stutter and a slip frame.

What is it about Dr. Shitansky's determination to know whatever it is she insists on knowing? It's like me right now, peering into and trying to describe this darkness that everyone can access at any time just by shutting their eyes. We both tell it the same thing: "Don't toy with me." But we're both wrong. The toying is all there is to it. The horizontal vertigo I feel as I lie here—knowing at any moment I could slide off the bed and through the door and along the surface of the earth, shoot out over the horizon and into space, pinned in place while the planet rolls out from under me—is all the wisdom and all the power.

I smell cigarettes somewhere. Who's smoking?

Out in the dark, the way I always felt like a spy without a country. I make reports to shadowy figures in dingy hallways and through battle-scarred pay phones. I meet contacts in 1940s automats and depressing 1970s cocktail lounges with would-be happy decor that only makes an all the more devastatingly grim impression of failure and pointlessness. That's me—just two sinister glowing eyes in a deep haze of unbearable sadness; get up and wade out into the dark looking for the black and white street, cough up cotton balls and wads of lint, strain to get even one lungful of crisp air, see the light wobble in potholes of rain.

I dream I run under a starry sky, my body weightless, flying, light as a spirit, my heart works, my lungs work, my legs...my legs work, everything works.

And I just run. My feet thud lightly on the cinder path and the dark sky over me blazes with stars all the way down to high mountain horizon and the shadow bulks of the peaks and slopes. Fly along forever, just like that, not running anywhere but here. From my bed I can see it, and I believe I know how it would feel, and it only makes where I am and who I am a burden. I know what I'm running from, though. A kitchen. An argument. Our last.

The room is almost suffocatingly close. Daladara sits with his back to the door, facing the window like a statue, hands poised over the abacus across his knees like a concert pianist. Every few seconds his fingers click the beads. He snaps a half-dozen in one sweep of his hand. He rides one bead with his left ring finger halfway down the line and keeps it there while his other fingers align the beads around it, all without any help from his eyes, which are riveted on a solitary cloud, framed in the window, traversing a broad panel of blue. Sweat drips from his face, soaks through his shirt and seeps out through his blazer. There are droplets of it on the tile around the chair's feet. Strangled words come writhing out between his teeth every so often. He's not speaking to me, or to anyone. I get the idea that he's naming different configurations on the abacus as they arise.

I sit down in one of the chairs behind him, pull out my little pocket notebook—official stationery, with serial number—and write down what I think he's saying. The moment I write a word down it's gone from my memory, replaced by the next one. It's weird. I have next to no memory at all of anything I wrote. Something about a dragon, I think...like a dragon of a certain color, in a certain compass direction, maybe? Upside down? And much more like that—images, red and gold, lacquered, black and silver, numbers, coordinates, simultaneous partial geometric transformations, flashes of acidic heat and arid cold.

"What the fuck are you doing?"

Daladara is staring at me, indignant.

"I was writing what you said," I say, lamely.

His eyes soften and a look of wonder comes into them.

"You wrote down...?"

He sets his abacus aside and holds out his hand, almost timidly, and I pass my notebook to him, open to that page. His face melts as he scans it, his breath bursts from him in a curt sigh and his eyes brim and spill over.

"I didn't get all of it," I say, feeling too stupid to say nothing and not smart enough to say nothing.

He looks up at me, his mouth folded.

"I thought I lost it...Thank you, man, holy shit! Can I keep this?"

"Sure."

He draws and exhales a long, wavering breath, and his body relaxes.

"Normally I would record that," he says after a minute. "But Shitansky won't allow it. I mean, I can't find a tape recorder."

"I can find you one," I say.

"Yeah? Thanks."

He's slumped back in his seat, exhausted, arms dangling, breathing through his mouth. He pinches his eyes, drags his palm across his face.

"Shit..." he sighs. Then smiles.

"I can't believe you got it, man! I can't believe it!"

He flips my little notebook, still pinched open between his right index finger and thumb.

"Why did you...?"

"I don't know," I say, a bit unsure how to respond to his strange gaiety and relief. "It just seemed like..."

"The thing to do," he says with a nod.

"Yeah, the thing to do."

"A little birdie told you."

"I don't know, something did."

His eyebrows draw slightly together.

"You've been around Shitansky when she's had her head in a hole, right? In the room?"

"Yeah, a few times."

He licks his lips, then nods.

"What? You think that did something to me?"

"Are you hearing things you haven't heard before?"

"I don't think so."

He shrugs.

"What were you doing?" I ask.

He takes a deep breath before he answers.

"Trying to describe that," he says.

He points to the cloud. White foam around pewter depths

limned in a thread of brilliant glare. From here, it seems as though it were just brushing the window frame, about to begin passing from view.

In my mind's eye, I see him do it, watching the cloud, monitoring the many clouds that make up that one cloud as they all but separate and then either melt back into the main bulk again or dissipate into straying fumes that become transparent and rejoin the blue instead. Did he watch every individual palpitating droplet and tally them, coarse or fine? Or was he looking for analog shapes in a blue and white inkblot? It isn't just blue and white, though, despite the evenness of the blue of the sky being no less arresting and strange, but the white is also grey, and a blaze of reflected sunlight that seems less like a color than a hueless gleam surrounding snowy prominences and blue dimples. All that goes on every moment as this one cloud crosses the sky, and Daladara, drenched in sweat, was trying to capture it all, sieve it through his abacus.

"Were you looking for something in particular? In the cloud?"

I notice how tired he is and I regret asking. It seems like a question that would take a lot of time and energy to answer. He just nods a little.

"I only know it if I see it," he says. "But I can't see it if I don't watch."

<hr>

Dr. Shitansky handles the money, literally. She has a safe full of cash in a storeroom with a specially-reinforced door, and on payday I have to stand outside and read off the amounts due while she counts out the money and stuffs it into labelled envelopes. Labelled by me, of course. Then Renbrui calls everybody in one by one, gives them their envelopes, and crosses their names off her to-pay list while I add them to my been-paid list. No banks, no checks, and certainly no digital money. We have a bi-weekly cash drop too, right out of an armored car. Renbrui collects it and we both count it independently. Per arrangement the deliveries come in slightly irregular amounts, never in nice even numbers. I guess this is supposed to be more secure, although I don't see how. Let's add it to the infinitely long list of things I don't understand.

Here I've been working with Renbrui all this time, and all I know about her is that she's a living impatience statue, who might debauch herself alone by the beach with cigarettes and whiskey. Nothing's ever quick enough for her. She never gets fully angry—not that I've seen—but she's always pinched and snapping her fingers and tapping her feet, and between the pinches and the squints and the snaps and the taps you get worn down very soon in her company. Her face is perennially set in a grim expression that repels small talk.

"Gross," she says behind me, making me jump. "We need you in the auditorium again. Corngholm says we overpaid him..."

She walks away, still talking, with the justified expectation that I will follow.

"...so we need Dr. Shitansky's confirmation on the amount. You have the ledger?"

I hold it up, proof of a fleeting presence of mind that's not very like me.

She glances at the ledger and swings on, guiding me back down through the maze to the center, where Dr. Shitansky sits bent forward in her seat, head inserted up to the temples through a hole in a thin sheet of suspended, copper-colored metal. Probably, copper. Renbrui waits, so I wait. Dr. Shitansky is like a tensed monument, listening with all her might. She seems ready to spring. Renbrui turns to me, hand out, to take the ledger, when a sharply-drawn breath draws our attention back to Dr. Shitansky.

Her brow is contracted, eyes squashed shut. She throws her head back, setting the metal sheet swaying. Her lips peel, exposing clenched teeth; her fingers squeeze the armrests so hard they creak.

I look at Renbrui in alarm. The hand she was holding out now turns to stay me, with a look that tells me not to interfere. After a moment, she asks—

"Dr. Shitansky?"

No response. Dr. Shitansky draws another rattling breath, her face spasming. One of her hands releases its grip and makes the cutting gesture. At once the swaying copper sheet rises and she sinks back in her seat, pawing her face with both hands. Renbrui stoops and locks eyes with her.

"Do—you—need—medical—assistance?" she asks, each word loud and distinct.

Dr. Shitansky doesn't seem to hear.

"Do—you—"

"Shh!" Dr. Shitanksy hisses. Her head droops forward, her body sags, her hands drop feebly into her lap.

"What happened?"

"Pain again," she answers after a moment. "What's he doing here?"

Her finger flicks at me.

"Accounts discrepancy."

"Ah," Dr. Shitansky says with a heavy nod. She stands abruptly, bracing herself on the arms of the chair, and sways for a second. Her knees lock, finally.

Another shuddering breath.

"We'll uh, look at that later. Right now, my maximum need is to know whether this really is hole-related pain, or if it's my brain. So we need someone else to sit, see if it happens to them. You're strong, Renbrui. Are you willing to try?"

"Yes," Renbrui says.

"It has to be now," Dr. Shitansky says, with a glimmer of gathering urgency. "Before current conditions change."

Renbrui summarily hands me her clipboard.

"Don't look at that," she says.

Then she sits down, without hesitation.

Dr. Shitansky waves to the booth and whoever's in there lowers the sheet around Renbrui's head. She sits bolt upright, palms down on her thighs, like a seated Pharoah, gazing impassively at the vacancy before her. The sheet comes down like a silent coronation. Dr. Shitansky pulls out a stopwatch the size of a small onion and clicks it sharply.

Tick-tick tick-tick tick-tick...

After a few minutes, Dr. Shitansky snaps the watch and the ticking stops. She gestures to the booth and the sheet of copper rises to hang in space over Renbrui's head.

"Anything?"

Renbrui reflects for a moment. Then shakes her head a little, almost with contrition.

Dr. Shitansky nods grimly.

"I see," she says. She pushes both hands through her sweaty hair and then lets them drop to her sides. "I see," she says again, resignedly. "I see."

Just now, out there, I hear three notes, like three pitches, sung pitches, sung by a choir...muffled but distinct notes, high, low, middle. Then no more.

Is it the rapture? Is it meant for just me to hear, to hearken me back to paradise, where I've always been from, but never been? In my happiest moments, there's a sad irony. If that irony made noise, it might sound like that.

A cricket, just one, chirps somewhere. I think it's inside the building.

My foot is starting to throb—get me out of here before it really gets going.

Strut down the street in an old suit and tie in oleaginous red orange and green colors from a low sky of luminous smoke we draw into our mind-lungs through invisible cigarettes, slow rolling colors pass around and down the street, like the undulations at the sea bottom, and the sourceless glare wavers in just the same way too. Move fast and slow, cock the right hand painfully stiff and spread like a kinked fan up to the face, rigid then soft, heavy and floating, high noon puddling my shadow under me in a barely discernible blue smudge, and it's in keeping with my way of life as a were-wizard. Keep it up. Push away. The polished steel frame of a doorway sails up around me; the dull cobalt gloom of a vinyl-booth coffee shop filled with palpitating smoke. I alight like a ghost on a stool at the counter and look at myself in a mirror that reflects a window, a panel of trembling color, orange turning purple turning brown. I can see myself, glassy-eyed and grinning from ear to ear, turn my coffee cup right side up on its saucer and then rotate its one ear round in 45 degree increments with my fingers more or less equally distributed around the brim. Like turning the knob on top of the radiator. A plume of smoke from an invisible cigarette trails from a spot about two inches from my mouth's left corner. My hair is soggy with cologne that trickles down my face. My suit is rumpled in gemlike facets; the featherweight fabric is sharkskin blue with a prismatic sheen that slides over me as I move beneath it. Oilslick suit. The people here are all otherwise invisible and the music sounds like it's being piped in via satellite and still barely decoupled from the omnipotent silence of outer space. Noonday sustains everyone here, so we all float in it like yolks in the egg, either here in this metal nightbox with its cool sticky counter top, everything from the clock on the wall to the coffee pot all in position since before the universe began around them, or out in the full albumin of the day street light, warping from color to color and oozing inside.

I'm here and not-here; I'm doing something more intense than imagining or dreaming—more intense, even, than waking. It's too intense for me maintain.

Was that you on the beach? Are you leading a double life, efficient at work, privately distraught?

It strikes me that it doesn't matter whether or not that person on the beach was you. The idea that you hide a violent, chaotic emotional life fits you too well. You would be incomplete without it now.

If I were younger, I would try to help you. Now though, while I want to help you, I know I can't.

You've already tried, other people have tried.

I can't deliberately help you, maybe no one can. It's possible, though, that I could help you accidentally. I could deliberately hang around, to try to make it happen.

A few days later there's some sort of event on the campus. I don't know anything about it. There's a banner set up, emblazoned with a big name just too far away for me to read. It's the wrong time of year for graduation. Considering all the formal wear, it might be a wedding, or a memorial service.

It's late in the day, the sun is behind the mountains and the light from the sky is now a lurid glow that doesn't touch the cooling earth. I feel the gloom afloat in the twilight, the air thrumming with a kind of ambient menace that saturates colors, deepens them, turns the shadows into buzzing hives, carries the sound of human voices farther and farther until everywhere you go you hear your own name being called, trailing after you like a phantom. The blossoms all open, the jasmine exhales into the wisteria, the breaths mingle and sink their colors in waves of brown-study wrapping human beings each in a nimbus that clings to them. It's mystery time—it never ends, we pass in and out of it. The shadow-light caught in the creases of the tree bark, the dangling strips of eucalyptus parchment, gathered in the long green sword-shaped leaves, the pale brown mesh of dead needles felting over the roots and stones. I don't see these things so much as they see me.

There's some kind of commotion now, something's happened. I hear a clamor of voices. I'm rushing through that uncannily diffuse, brown air. Among those other voices is a shrill, anguished scream.

"Nooo! Nooo!"

I see her there—Renbrui's on the ground, lying half in and half out of the doorway to the Institute. I can hear her moaning, and for a moment I mistake what she's lying in for a pool of blood, but it's not, it's a sort of viscous perspiration streaming off of her, visibly welling out of her hands and face. People surround her barking orders at each other, talking about lifting her head or stuffing a wallet in her mouth, and she's all but doubled backwards, eyes rolling, mouth working, hair soaked, a flow of thick water that beads and wells in the corrugations of her sweater, hands kinked like talons, rigid, bent as far as her wrists will go, spasms.

"Jesus," I say.

Her lungs heave and push out long screams.

A woman who works in the hamburger place by the campus—I forget her name, Angela something—is kneeling down beside Renbrui when she suddenly unbends, stops howling. She looks around, bewildered, like a little girl waking up from a bad dream. Tears cut tracks through the gummy sweat on her face. They drop in straight lines from her tired eyes, down slack, disinterested features. She raises her hands as if they were unbearably heavy, presses her forehead and cheeks into them, then pushes the dampness back up into her hair.

"Are you all right?" Someone asks.

She's beyond hearing, I think. With delicacy, she turns her body and begins to stand. Something tells me it would be especially wrong to touch her now, to offer her support, even if she needs it. She's as fragile as a soap bubble. Very gently, she takes hold of the hard metal door frame with her left hand, stabilizing herself as she straightens up. Her back is to us. She steps into the building, holding herself stiffly against the weight of her sweat-drenched clothes.

"Do you want me to find you something dry?"

That's me, asking that. She stops, turns her whole body and looks at me. Mouth open. Not blinking. Then she nods, once. Turns. Resumes. She's heading for the bathroom off the lobby. In theory, anyone can use it, but she made it essentially her private reserve by bringing in her own supply of little fancy scented soaps carved to look like red flowers, yellow birds, purple plums, and orange fish. She stocks the place with her own pink hand towels, a doily on the toilet tank, and a glass jar of potpourri with a pewter top.

I hurry to Renbrui's office, fill my arms with some of the garments hung up on the coat rack, and rush back to her in a cloud of her fragrance.

I knock at the bathroom door.

"Leave them."

"What, uh—on the floor?"

"...Leave them."

The next day Dr. Shitansky calls me into her office and tells me that I'll have to be taking over some of Renbrui's duties. As she's detailing them, "some" sounds more and more like "all," but then she mentions that I'll also be getting a commensurate raise in salary effective immediately. I only ask her what this means for Renbrui, if she's being let go.

"Renbrui is of maximum importance to us right now," Dr. Shitansky tells me. In her left hand she takes three walnuts from one of the wooden bowls on her desk and cracks them in her fingers. She picks out the meats, then dumps the shell fragments into the empty wooden bowl.

"The experience she had yesterday is hole-related, in my opinion. This calls for a change. So from now on she will be a non-academic fellow of the Institute. You'll find the enrollment documentation in the personnel file marked 'intake,' form 082. Do your own form while you're at it. Form 15d. You're Clerical Associate Gross from now on. Your first responsibility in your new capacity will be to search for and hire a nurse for Renbrui."

She raises her right index finger and says, "Priority one."

What did I see there? That sorrow and rage. Pure. Stronger than she was. She was strong enough to have feelings stronger still than she was. Too strong for herself. I knew she reminded me of her, now I see the essence. It's beautiful. It's noble. And it's always only a moment away from death.

That night, Dr. Shitansky interviews Renbrui, staying late. The old website was retired once we were fully staffed, so I have to earn my new salary by composing the notification for a nurse and preparing it for distribution without the assistance of anything more electronic than a desk lamp. When, at last, I'm done, the night outside is deep and well underway. A ribbon of black lies between the Institute and the parking lot. As I move out into it, begin to cross it, seeing what's around me only as it is silhouetted against the distant lights, I glance back and see Dr. Shitansky in profile at her desk with Bas beside her, and I know that Renbrui is in the chair facing her across the desk, just out of my sight. Dr. Shitansky is piloting the Institute like a lone mariner, out into the unknown. Throw the word out into silence, wait for it to rebound, forming a momentary zone just long enough for an adroit listener to drive over, running across the sky using fireworks as stepping stones. You'd better keep moving, because that spark is about to go out, and the next one is already popping. There'd better be another spark where you're throwing your foot. Sooner or later there won't be, but more likely you'll get caught up short looking at something and forget to step altogether. Then, down.

Daladara drapes his palm over the back of his neck and sweeps it up to the crown of his head before letting go with a "Damn it." I watch his hands pull out and light a cigarette with that white lighter; he grimaces around the first drag as if the tobacco were foul, rucks his forehead as he pours the used smoke out in a straight gale. His eyes tick along the floor tiles, as if he were moving an imaginary bead along their edges. Maybe he can't help it, and the calculation is always going on in his mind like a numbers station rattling away at the frontiers of radio.

"I should have been there," he says. "What the hell *stopped* me?"

"You think you would have seen something that everyone else missed?"

"Oh, I *know* I would have. No doubt."

He sighs.

"No doubt about that."

"Like what?"

He shakes his head.

"Sign, some kind. At least, I could have said something about what was doing it, maybe why. Why her."

"You know she put her head in the hole, right?"

"No," he says, only now raising his eyes to look at me. "I didn't know that. That makes some kind of sense, though. Did Shitansky know, or was she just winging it?"

"She told her to do it. Dr. Shitansky did. She'd just finished a session, and it was looking like it was hurting her. So she asked Renbrui to try it, right there and then, before conditions could change."

"What happened?"

"She just sat for a bit, until Dr. Shitansky ended it. Maybe, five minutes?"

"That's got to be it," he says. "It just hit her differently."

"Listen," I say. "Someone like her—she's too strong for that. If it...gets...*to* her..."

He's looking at me with surprise on his face, and I shut up.

From then on Renbrui *was* different. If she had been cold before, she was even colder now, but she no longer had her former way of mastering every situation, or seeming to, and her manner had utterly lost that almost jaunty beleaguered quality it once had. Now instead there's a greater mobility and vehemence around her mouth, I can almost see icy fumes drop from the corners of her lips, and a kind of unworld shadow falls over her eyes so that they seem to glint out from a somber obscurity, making me think of flames reflected in gold pillars, trembling blue geysers of fragrant smoke rising from huge heaps of incense, a band of violet and orange sunset under a heavy ceiling of saturated purple clouds like a dying hearth in a dark room, an eerie noise of discordant, plaintive music that just misses the air and calls after her so that she always seems to be hearkening to sounds and voices no one else can hear. She would snatch up the receivers from telephones that hadn't rung to listen for a while, her face blank, her eyes hooded and unavailable, then she would set the receiver quietly down into its cradle again with a subtle adjustment to her expression that made it seem as though she were about to smile a little. The original Renbrui, the one I met first, kept most of herself out of sight behind a professionally-impersonal briskness and efficiency, but you could tell there was some sort of person there. The intended effect actually depended on your realizing that, so that you too would lock away your personality like an untidy bedroom. Now, though, it's as if the hidden side has become virtual, pulling in all the power of secret pivots and hidden analogies, because she brought something back out of the hole, carries it around with her, and consults with it like an abstract familiar. Maybe it answers her questions, but I think it's more likely they commune together in mute, shared concentration, like two people listening to a piece of music together. In this case, it's the unmusic of the unworld they bask in, like undead plants in moonlight, august and spectral, in a sublime condition, half-dematerialized in revisitation of a special past that holds all the answers in abeyance, stunned, not knowing what word is to come next, filled—suffused with expectancy and longing, hieratic and somber...I'm just in love with her, all right? That's not what this is about so forget it, the way I forgot.

Dr. Shitansky's interviews with her go on well into the night. I'm leaving late, turn and see the light on her office, Dr. Shitansky in profile at her desk with Bas beside her, and I know that Renbrui is in the chair facing her across the desk, just out of my sight. It's like Dr. Shitansky is taking the institute out to sea like a lone mariner...

Back to the auditorium with today's messages. There's a man I haven't seen before, sitting in the corner. Dr. Shitansky passes me on her way to the booth, stops, turns back to me, indicates the man, says, "This is my father," then proceeds about her business. The man doesn't seem old enough to be her father, or perhaps I should say it the other way, that she seems too old to be this man's daughter. Their only readily noticeable physical similarity is that they're both people with impressively large heads. His is masterly. He looks like Will Quadflieg. Both he and she have the same high, cerebral foreheads; his is emphasized by a receding hairline, with a white tuft in front of each ear. A broad, aquiline nose, a pouting mouth, and dark, slightly protuberant eyes. He keeps his chin lowered and his hands in his lap, fingers sticking out any old way. A black corduroy blazer with very wide lapels, a laddered shirt down to a belt hitched over a small gut. He's like a human owl; he sits practically without moving anything but his head, looking around and visibly swallowing. He could be either highly intelligent or completely loony. When he does finally speak, his voice is sonorous and powerful, without any trace of hoarseness.

"What happens now?" he asks Dr. Shitansky.

She responds with an upraised hand and turns to me, holding a shallow cardboard box in her hand. She passes the box to me, and I see it has a couple of audio cassettes sliding around in it.

"Transcribe these for me, Gross," she says. "Maximum priority. And when you're done, erase them. Make two copies of the transcript first. Oh, uh, this is Clerical Associate Gross, father."

"How do you do?" he says continentally.

Inside the booth, the membrane vibrates with taped information and auditory signals projected on a uranium nerve. Renbrui looks over at me, opens her mouth and says "ah ah ah." She's discouraging me from doing or thinking something, but I don't what. I have no real idea what she means at all, but her sly expression makes me think that maybe she just wanted to throw me. That sort of mischievousness isn't like her.

Dr. Shitansky turns to me once more, just as she's leaving. "Blank those tapes."

RENBRUI: Turn.

DR. SHITANSKY: [still adjusting her microphone for the beginning of the session, says something unintelligible over microphone scuff and bump]

RENBRUI: Turn so let me expound what's bowed your shoulder and paled your cheek.

DR. SHITANSKY: All right. This is our first interview, Dr. Shitansky and Renbrui—

RENBRUI: Renbrui...

DR. SHITANSKY:—uh Thursday January 13 2022, 3:47 PM, TISH. Uh, my office. Renbrui, will you please describe for me your experience during our experiment last Friday?

RENBRUI: I will shut down anyone who tries to save her.

DR. SHITANSKY: Renbrui, could you describe what happened during the experiment please?

RENBRUI: I will snipe anyone who helps.

DR. SHITANSKY: Please describe what happened during the experiment.

RENBRUI: Of course...Of course.

DR. SHITANSKY: Take your time.

RENBRUI: Of course...

DR. SHITANSKY: Think about what you saw, what you heard, what you felt...Did you see anything? Did you hear anything? Did you feel anything? No matter how small.

RENBRUI: Of course.

DR. SHITANSKY: No matter how small, Renbrui.

RENBRUI: You know fucking well what I'm going to see and hear, Shitansky—it's pain. Pain and death.

DR. SHITANSKY: Set aside psychological considerations and focus.

RENBRUI: Psychological considerations!

DR. SHITANSKY: Focus on concrete physical sensations—

RENBRUI: Psychological...

DR. SHITANSKY:—concrete sensations not originating in your personality.

RENBRUI: My personality!

DR. SHITANSKY: Concrete sensations that are unaccountable, that are received from any external source. Any source external to you. Renbrui. Renbrui. Renbrui. Any concrete sensation. Renbrui. Focus.

RENBRUI: Pain and death. Everybody turns around a...we lost.

DR. SHITANSKY: Explain.

RENBRUI: Can't explain, nothing there. Nothing to explain.

DR. SHITANSKY: What does everybody turn around?

RENBRUI: Lost...lostness. Losts. Losts. Losts!

DR. SHITANSKY: I'm sitting right beside you, Renbrui. Shouting isn't necessary.

RENBRUI: I command you to return to your proper form!

DR. SHITANSKY: I can hear you when you speak at a normal level—

RENBRUI: I order you—!

DR. SHITANSKY: Stop shouting.

RENBRUI: I ord—I order you to return to your correct form!

The nurse she hires to watch over Renbrui is a sturdy young man with a dry red complexion, sun-dazzled eyes, a thick sinewy throat and a plume of of blonde curls piled on top of his head. His hoarse voice will sometimes skate off into a dry rasping whisper for a moment before dropping back to tone, as if he's been shouting. He'd responded to the posting the day it was put up, and he had very little competition at that. I'm not sure what he does, exactly, apart from trying to take her vitals. She won't let him touch her.

I ask Daladara if he can diagnose her problem.

"You say she said 'I order you to return to your true form'?"

"Correct form. Actually, first she said 'proper,' then 'correct.'"

"Could mean anything."

"Dr. Shitansky thought she was talking to someone she'd made contact with through the hole."

"What do you think? I didn't hear it."

"It sounded to me like she was parodying Dr. Shitansky back to her."

"Like Dr. Shitansky was ordering her to get back in shape?"

"That's what it sounded like to me."

"So it was like she felt she was losing her shape?"

"Could be. She didn't sound much like herself. It was like it was something she'd heard before."

"You think she could have been quoting a movie or something?"

"Only if it was a movie she'd really internalized."

He consults his abacus.

"Well," he says, "I can't tell you anything except that there's nothing here that gives us any reason to think that what seems obvious isn't true. I could try again a little later, sometimes a second pass will turn something up, but I got a set up to do now."

"What do you mean?"

"I do set ups from time to time. It's a lot of fun. More fun than sit ups."

His clients hire him to do these set-ups. The idea is that he has a special way of investigating someone, to make sure they're "on the level." The way he describes it, it's like a supernatural background check, to see in advance if someone is worth doing business with, and what kind of business, and if they can be trusted, and with what, and how far. It's a form of bet-hedging with an abacus and geomantic calculations. He can't tell me about his set up this afternoon, but he describes a former occasion, to give me a sense of what's involved.

A friend drops him off downtown on what Daladara presented to her as a benign errand. The moment she's out of sight, "straight to mission face," Daladara says. He has a printout of the mark's picture, and he knows where he parks. So he walks to the parking structure, walks inside, walks up ramps from level to level until he reaches the second topmost, then walks purposively to and fro, pantomiming a search. If anyone bugs him about what he's doing there, he'll say he lost his phone and he's looking for it. He always keeps an eye on spot eight three. Here comes the basic white SUV. Spot eight three. Daladara lunges down and picks up nothing off the ground, his back to the cameras, then heads for the exit, tucking nothing into his jacket pocket and carrying himself like an impatient man running late. He waits downstairs for his mark to go by, then follows him across the pedway and into the building. His mark says hi to the woman at the security desk and passes on to the elevators. Daladara swings up, waves his unopened electricity bill, simultaneously telling her he has a delivery for his mark's law firm, legal courier, and gets waved into the same elevator. Now they're side by side. Punch the floor right below his. His mark is on his phone of course. Daladara pulls out a few coins and puts the application on a gold Sacagawea dollar with a few dials of his finger and something from the paper packet in his jacket pocket, then drops the whole handful, scattering coins on the floor.

"Shit!" he says through his teeth, bending to pinch up each coin. The doors separate. He leaves, apparently forgetting the gold dollar. He takes the stairs two at a time and gets to the mark's destination floor just as he's emerging from the elevator. Hurry over, guy's still on his phone, thrust an arm between the closing doors so they jostle and reluctantly heave back—the dollar is gone. Daladara snaps his fingers and looks around. Now who could have taken that dollar...?

He waits five minutes in the men's room, then heads for the law office. While he was in the toilet stall he'd gently pried open his power bill, extracted the envelope's contents, replaced them with some blank pages torn from his notebook and invisibly indicted with certain indicators correlated with the patterns he strikes on his pocket abacus, and then resealed the envelope. Good enough to fool a camera at the far end of the hall. Now he delivers the envelope, under the door, and gets away, back to the stairwell, round and round and round, down to the ground. He waves to Ms. Security and then he's out into the zoom of the street in the first hours of night time.

A bit of a walk, he thinks, and then dinner at Norm's. Feeling all right, but of course the real bringdown still has to be done, and that can always backfire no matter how good a set up goes.

I ask him if that one backfired. He says he's not sure yet.

A momentary lull between chores. For a little while anyway, there's nothing left to tabulate collate file or copy. But my foot is troubling me, I'm afraid to stand up, so I just send my gaze down the gleaming, dark TISH corridor in front of me, frail sun on the greenery outside, air conditioning on my face. It's like the old department stores, I remember, where the smell of the corn dogs from the Orange Julius in the food court struggles in vain to penetrate the Maybelline fog of the cosmetics department, muted quaalude brass winding everything down like a valium rave. I was condemned in food court, and torn down. My spot still stands empty; not even weeds grow there now, nothing there but the weight of my cheek propped on my fist and the gravity dragging my eyes down to stare at the rubberized grey-black desk top cluttered with antique office gear. I've got nobody to think about, not even a cat. I've got someone not to think about.

The squawk box in front of me crackles. Out of it comes Dr. Shitansky's voice murmuring, "Secre-hem—Clerical Associate Gross, would you come into my office now please."

In Dr. Shitansky's office I find her, Bas, Dr. Shitansky, and

Dr. Corngholm. He's an elusive mythic enigma like Bigfoot or the Loch Ness Monster; this is the first time I've been this close to him. Previously, I'd only ever sighted him chatting with Allegre, toe always tapping in the same slow tempo that never wavered, a brown sack of plain ham and cheese sandwiches on his knee, blithe and high and aloof and slow swimming underwater gestures. From what I can make out in the reports I type up, his project involves the creation of linguistic exercises designed to recreate thinking patterns of dead languages. He calls it "preserving thoughtways." Allegre tells me that he keeps a bunch of different water bottles somewhere, each at a different PH level, and drinks them in a fixed rotation depending on time of day. He also evidently jogs an incredible distance to and from the institute. Or was it bicycling he did? Now it's like I'm seeing him for the first time, and he doesn't seem as large. There's a sort of brown film over his head, like a smudge on the lens of life or whatever, that makes his Hapsburg face sort of smokey and vague. I get a firm handshake from him, a bright smile and a very intensely blue gaze, like he's scanning me.

I'm nervous. It's difficult to connect the snarling, tortured voice I'd heard on the tapes with the woman with the clipboard, standing there, totally together. Is all that still there inside her, contained for right now, or did it just pass through and leave again? Does she know I heard those tapes? Now I'm really frightened. I don't dare look in her direction, but if I avoid looking, that's something else out of the ordinary for her to notice. If she does know, I can't look at her. If she doesn't know, my looking at her might give it away, but so would assiduously not looking at her. I have to manage my looks.

We all have to go outside and see this surveying equipment Dr. Corngolm's set up. He says it's designed to make distinct linguistic microclimates visible. He and Dr. Shitansky are very caught up in it, very into it, and their exchanges are impossible for me to follow, which is too bad, because I'm supposed to be taking all of it down in steno. What does it have to do with holes? Well, pulling thoughtways out of the hole of time, I guess.

Pulling mindflavors from the airwaves. That presupposes that what is undiscovered is in a kind of hole, which, I guess, dovetails with Dr. Shitansky's theories.

I can't see where it's coming from—a grating, mournful noise that gets a little louder, and I realize it's Renbrui making it. She's crushed her mouth and eyelids shut as though she were trying to hold vomit down. Then her features shiver apart and relax into a withered, tormented expression. Her eyes brim with tears that overflow down her cheeks. I say her name. She doesn't acknowledge me. The noise dithers in her throat, like it can't decide whether or not to come out. She sort of flails then, bends around with angular hands for a second, then takes off down the slope with a yelp of pain. It all happens too fast. Before I can respond, she's halfway to the concrete path down there, hair and skirt tossing in the wind like a flame wildly guttering, and Dr. Shitansky pelts after her. There's a swimming pool down that way, I think, and my scalp bristles.

Weeks of idle wandering around the campus have taught me that you can reach the pool area faster if you avoid the pedestrian underpass leading and just cut across the street, provided the cars don't get you. So I'm already there when Renbrui emerges, clutching at the air, her clothes, eyes bulging, mouth working, and I can hear the reverberant slamming of Dr. Shitansky's feet as she pounds up after her. Renbrui dashes past me, easily eluding my attempts to stop her, and is about to fling herself over the rail and into the pool when Dr. Shitanksy, shooting out like a rocket, grabs hold of her. She throws an arm around her waist and clamps her to her side. Panting, Dr. Shitansky turns and carries Renbrui up the slope, tucked into her armpit like a bolt of carpet. Her stern, scarlet face drips perspiration, and locks of her hair are glued to her cheeks and broad forehead. Renbrui writhes and bends like a fish out of water, her discomposed face is barely recognizable. Her mouth works, but nothing comes out.

"Get that door open!" Dr. Shitansky roars at me.

I pull the door wide and follow them into the institute. Dr.

Shitansky takes Renbrui into her office, throws her down on the sofa, points her index finger in Renbrui's face, and says—

"Now you calm down!"

Renbrui cackles. She tries to get up. Dr. Shitansky kneels on the floor by the sofa and presses her back down with one hand.

Renbrui struggles, and her contortions transform her laughter into an inhuman warble. The moment her breath is exhausted, the hand on her chest suddenly shoves down hard, preventing the expansion of her ribcage. Her mouth and eyes open together. She gasps for breath, and her struggle becomes a frenzy. Then the hand lifts a little and she draws air greedily and vocally, adding a kind of snarl as if she were trying to speak. The hand on her chest suddenly clamps like a vice on her jaw.

"You remember you're a straight shooter, Renbrui," Dr. Shitansky says.

Renbrui's discoordinated features slacken into a derisive grin, but, with only a slight movement of her hand, Dr. Shitansky gives her a shake that makes her body flop against the sofa like a doll.

"I *said—remember—*you're a *straight—shooter!*"

Dr. Shitansky squeezes Renbrui's throat, lifting the watch on her right wrist up before her eyes. After a moment she slackens her grip, and Renbrui snarls, giggles, lunges, barks half-formed insults at her.

"Three...four...five...six..."

Dr. Shitansky counts aloud, impassively. When she reaches thirty, she closes her grip again and restarts her count at one. When she reaches thirty, she slackens her grip, Renbrui sucks air, begins to snarl and swear, and over her voice Dr. Shitansky chants the seconds in monotone, then strangles at thirty. This is repeated, many times. When I finally tear my eyes away to check, the clock on the wall has advanced forty minutes.

"You made it worse," Daladara says.

"I don't want any fooling around," Dr. Shitansky says.

"You'll have plenty of fooling around to deal with if you take that line with her now," Daladara retorts.

Dr. Shitansky somehow manages to relax her brow and transfer her vehemence directly to her pale eyes.

"I *said* I don't want any fooling around!" Her voice is level.

"I know that, but this isn't the way to avoid it." The patient advisor.

"Renbrui is going to have to learn," Dr. Shitansky says. "That's all."

"If she could learn, she would—"

"Haven't I said, that's all?"

———

Well up out of shallow sleep into a kind of deeply unconscious wakefulness. It's night time, in a dark room. Quiet. My own labored breathing. Dull, relentless pain in my foot and leg. Occasional spasms. I'm so tired it's like each spasm takes a whole minute to go up my leg, peter out above my knee somewhere. Mouth open, eyes open, hands empty. So many hours on my back; the sad, wasted, stagnant feeling, turning to mush. It's sickening lying here, going slacker and slacker. The foot of my bed, the room—a dry laugh, not mine. Or was it something outside? Something that's having a laugh?

The opposite wall had been lost in the murky half-darkness of this room at night, but now it's orange with sunset light coming from I don't know where, but it moves over the door and onto the other wall as I turn my head feebly to look. I'm breathing harder.

I see a bathtub there, and a mannequin in it, being bathed by arms that reach out of the dark, like astronaut arms, with bulky white sleeves and gloves. They dip their sponges in acrid white water that runs clear down her sides, crush their sponges against her stern wooden face and neck, her stomach and hips. Not in the room but around the edges of the orange sunset light

there's a pink twilight sky and the silhouettes of desert brambles. No sound but my breathing, and the steady trickling. No
feeling but drunken pain, wisdom, wise memories of longing,
hate for wisdom, disgust with this thing lying here, not wanting
to be free, those unhurried hands wash the dummy, water drib-
bles from the saturated sponges, I can hear the faint noise each
sponge makes as hands press it to the awkward and immobile
body lying in a white serum and accomplish nothing apart from
striating its sides with transparent ropes of water that expand
and vanish back into the flesh of the bath. No smell apart from
my own stale body, breath and bedclothes, no bath steam in the
bone-dry air. Decades that I can feel separate me from that
panel of sunset light over there. Something is happening in the
bathtub. To her. The wooden hand reaches for something silver
that flashes orange in the light.

I have to shut my eyes, but now what do I see? A round
table in a little familiar kitchen in the brown light of late afternoon, a pink stone heart pendant without a chain lying in a dish
of golden oil, and such a strong feeling of remembering a person,
a love, a beauty I knew about once. A dry laugh, not mine, I
open my eyes, the opposite wall is lost in half-murky darkness of
night in this room, breathing harder.

I know I won't get it back. Even if I did, I wouldn't have it. I
already have it. That is, I had it. Now, I have the memory of it.
There's no way to have any more. I have only the finishing of it.
The finished. The gone.

Who laughed? I heard laughter—who was that, laughing?
What's so funny? It's not me, though.

I look up from my embarrassingly messy new ledger and
Renbrui is just coming around the corner.

"Dr. Shitansky says we're going on a little trip," she says.
The steely note that used to underpin her every word is
completely gone. Now her voice has a hollow elfshot quality,

every bit as firm, but the words seem to bypass the ear and bite directly into the brainstem.

"You'll be taking dictation," she tells me in that same spectral way, leading me to the car.

Renbrui sits ramrod-straight in the driver seat. I'm looking at Dr. Shitansky, asking her with my eyes if she really is allowing Renbrui to drive. It seems nearly every moment one or the other of her hands will leave the steering wheel to tap an illuminated yellow indicator on one of what must be ten different control panels distributed all around her, even above her head. Over her shoulder, I can see a dash readout that consists of nothing but countless fluctuating two, three, four, or five digit numbers, all vivid yellow in individual black glass wafers. It's like a space ship. The personalized seat adjustment and climate control panel in the armrest beside me has about a dozen little windows, and a long narrow keypad. We've been driving for about ten minutes and Dr. Shitansky is still punching the keys in hers.

The ride is silent. The window has a tint modification function that you operate by touching a partitioned section of the glass, which draws yellow rings around each of my fingertips and spells out little messages like "continue steady to darken, pulse pressure to stipple." I don't dare change anything.

"Take this down," Dr. Shitansky says abruptly. "These are column headings. Consistency, latency, identity...solidity...and rights."

I get that down and sit waiting with my pen poised. Landscape sluices past Dr. Shitansky's profile, one elbow on the arm rest, arm up, index finger pointing. She folds up her finger and lowers her arm. I guess that was it.

Neon lights up on the ridge line, looking pale and out of place against the dull pearl overcast. Crevasses between the ridges flash us views of the illuminated golden grid of the city, lights that melt through the smoke of twilight and seem about to detach from the intangible shadow buildings they belong to.

"Take this down," Dr. Shitansky says. "Side note. Decongestants are toxic for cats. No decongestant ingredient."

I scribble the words.

Renbrui navigates through traffic with perfect, mechanical steadiness. There is no perceptible acceleration or braking. Every now and then, with a smooth dip of her left hand, she triggers the clicking turn signal and we float into a different lane. Red and white lights carousel around the car in a kind of numb ballet, and I can hear Dr. Shitansky's breath whistling in her nostrils, the ride's so quiet.

"Underline the words where it says, 'no decongestant,'" Dr. Shitansky says.

I make an emphatic pen stroke.

The car swoops us up an offramp. We roll along a broad avenue. Identical supermarket parking lots with little parasitic shopping centers drift past at five minute intervals.

"Take this down," Dr. Shitansky says. "The world hole leaks. What is its nature? Can it be perceived as such? There is no *one* experiment for this. Underline one. Now read that back to me."

I'm up to "perceived" when the car jolts to a sudden stop.

Dr. Shitansky shouts, Renbrui is already getting out of the car, through my window I see her unbending, her smile makes a tight scarlet angle over those wan white icy little teeth in bright gleaming red gums and a half-invisible veil of frost—

—a still-smoking crater where the opposite lane used to be, and the end of a city bus protruding from it, smashed to shikes, smouldering, like war wreckage.

I follow her to the rim, look down into it at the sheets tangled around my feet pressed against the baseboard, and then to the bare white wall opposite me, and then again along my body and down into the hole in my memory, reminding me of the time I tried to remember something and couldn't. Nothing but stale wind where voices should be; I'm in the wrong place to hear them, not where I should be, as usual, I never am, but in the hole at the center of the emergency. All prepositions and no places, and no times. I'm in the at of the toward beneath, but here's the moment a brusque voice barks.

Renbrui's turning that direction. A dreamy look comes into her face. She's raising a pistol in her hand. My left foot throbs, tremors dart up my leg like fleeting vacancies, a wisp of cold wind blows a dissolving odor of gunpowder around me. Is it the same pain that comes with a bullet wound? I wouldn't know. I *wouldn't*. If she shot anyone, it wasn't me.

I'm walking beneath automated trains on elevated lines, their baleful lights mired in tepid gunsmoke, roll by overhead like marine shadows...No, this isn't it. This isn't the end of that memory, the street lined with black glass cars, dim dash lights and cigarette cherries behind their tinted windows—this isn't the end of the memory by the crater, the pain by the crater, and the fire, and the bus—great chasms of darkness across the city in staggered outages, a disjointed voice on a PA system. That's not it. That's not the memory. I don't want to remember.

Walking, am I the only one? It's not the right kind of night for Los Angeles. So is that where I am? I can see the dark towers of downtown clustered together, the ominous spires standing in the distance like so many passive beacons of menace, propping up the ceiling of fear. Someone lying sick and scared in bed somewhere is listening to my footsteps. It's Los Angeles, but with the wrong night on it.

You should be scared, buddy, I think. I'm not looking for you, but if I find you...

I'm not going to stop walking, and if I keep walking, sooner or later, I will find you, and when I do: nothing and everything, everything and nothing. Everybody knows what happens to you when you meet *you*. I'm not looking for you, but I'm coming, just the same.

I turn at the corner, more to avoid crossing the street than to take myself anywhere special. There's no traffic, the streets might as well be movie sets, but crossing the street would tend to confirm that. I have nowhere special to go, not anymore. I used to. Then she—

I don't want to break this by making it too obviously a set up. I don't want to go where breaking this would send me. So keep on walking, not a care in the world, turn the corner again, stay in the fiction, just stay in the fiction, no special place, no she, no bathtub—the block doesn't change, the wind doesn't blow, there's no city noise. It's like I'm putting on a little show for that frightened, listening ear in a bed of pain up there, somewhere, but as I turn a corner—who was that? I hear a sharp inhalation of breath. Like a gasp of pain, sudden pain, the sound someone makes when they've just cut themselves—it wasn't me, you, or anyone, but it suffuses the reverse of the world. It shakes me like an earthquake and I'm suddenly weak, very weak.

It's gone now, just as completely as an earthquake goes away. You remember that you went through it, but the moment itself is a blur. You can never forget what you can't remember. You can't forget what you weren't present to see. I'm frightened. I realize, out here in the street with nowhere to go, no one to go to, that you and I are both frightened, terrified, not of each other —it's already too late to learn its rules. If it has any rules.

There's an accident up there. Ribbons of black fire twist from rents in a wrecked bus that's fallen forward into what must be a sinkhole. The asphalt cracked open, exposed soil like rotten cake, the front end of the bus is submerged in standing water as viscous as oil. Gunsmoke pours from broken windows, stinging my eyes and catching my lungs, but the fire gives off almost no heat. I look down again into the crater at my feet writhing under the covers, a siren in the street, the sound goes on and on, draws no nearer, never fades. They must be dead by now, the ambulance has been coming for so long. The far wall dims, maybe a cloud is traversing the moon. In time, the light, pale as it is, will return. A soft voice speaking calmly, downstairs it sounds like. A breeze plunges into the treetops and sets all the leaves whirring; the branches dip and the petals spin in the light like infinite sequins, a luminous living pale green swims in the mineral blue and white, the glory that descends in a cataract all around me is almost oppressive, a green and brown landscape of ridges and canyons, trees, vines, and blossoming shrubs, pungent herbs, sweet grasses, a mercurial perfume from all the flowers, birdsong, a humming music that never entirely fades without ever becoming fully distinct, and everywhere I see shining embodied perspectives adorned with broken seals, all framing this crater, the burning bus, the spinning, tumbling flames, the gouts of smoke. Here in the fractured shade and coolness of the live oaks next to blacking out in the immemorial perfume and murmur of shining embodied perspectives as they turn their eternal youth and splendor on me, the joy ripping me apart.

Turn aside, down out of the way, a worn brown leaf-lined groove leads me through grey-trunked live oaks and among the vestiges of fallen trees all but melted back into the ground like low beds scattered everywhere. I'm running away. I'm keeping that crater behind me.

This is a hushed place, a short cut. The slope rushes my feet beneath me so I hurry along without meaning to, and I am accompanied by others I can't see, like many little ones trotting near me, lightly over the mold and through the brambles. Fair folk. The ground levels out. I slow to a walk again, and my coterie recedes without disappearing. My every move is watched, and knowing this this makes me clumsy. Through a break in the foliage I see down into a broad open valley, its edges sloping gently down to a distinct, pale brown crease at the bottom.

A little white thread follows the crease like a needle in a groove. Jagged, wan shadows shear and fade behind the low shrubs and rocks scattered around the valley floor with each flash of the thread as it comes.

The sight of that thread petrifies me. I couldn't get away, could I? I can't run. I shut my eyes. It's still there. Everything in me resists the idea that I could turn my back to it. I back away. I can't take my eyes from it—I don't dare.

The thread keeps making its way along the crease down there, and I know it won't stop, it's always moving, always coming, on the way. Even when I've backed far enough away that I can no longer see it, I still keep facing it. I'm alone now, with it. It spins and jerks and travels.

Pain shooting up my leg, throbbing my foot like a piece of broken glass wedged between the bones. The pain has worn me out. I throw off a sheet heavy with my sweat, claw at my chest. I can't breathe. My head rises and falls with my inhalations and exhalations, my mouth hangs open. I drag myself off the bed and across the floor to the window, try to drive it up, open, I want to shove my head outside and suck air.

But, the window is already open. The night air is tepid, thick, disgusting. It oozes over the sill and down into the room like poison. I have to do something. What can I do. I can lie here, my leg screaming, my face mashed to the floor.

I remember leaving the hospital, numbly returning to my place and taking a seat in my chair. My father said "this pistol's just a long-distance hole punch" when I asked him why he didn't keep it at home. Just a game of target practice. The vanquished enemy is a battalion of nice sturdy sheets of paper, each one with its own shapeless constellation, stacked away in manila folders in a steel file cabinet that smelled lightly of gunsmoke when you slid open the drawer.

I sat in my chair awaiting orders as usual, not receiving any as usual. Feathers of gunsmoke from a hole, strings writhing out from the black brane to catch me, strictly in keeping with natural laws, followed by a silence that's dense, fraught, like a massing wave that swells without curling or frothing, just getting steadily taller.

—Hospital...why? What was I doing in the hospital? Something happened, then—recovery room, blue curtains, a needle sticking out the back of my hand, my arm sticking out of a wan hospital smock, nurses around. I'm reeling forward, my vision swimming, I'm dizzy, I can't breathe, it's like my ribcage has been blown open and can't close, can't drive the old air out and draw new air in. The nurses are all talking at once, telling me I'm OK, one of them says she's giving my fentanyl through the IV.

"I can't breathe!" a voice is shouting. My voice. A hand draws the curtain aside and Dr. Shitansky's huge face lunges in at me. I stop struggling. I pant for breath.

"You had an *accident*, Mr. Gross," she says. "An *accident*. You are in a hospital right now. You have been examined. Your life is not in danger. You are not seriously injured."

I can't feel my foot, I can't see it.

"There is zero indication of any physical problem that could cause respiratory difficulties. Your trouble breathing is emotional in nature."

We stopped. We got out of the car. There was a bus in a hole, and on fire. There was something about Renbrui and a gun? All I can come up with is the image of the three of us approaching the crater, the burning—bus? our concern, the rim of the hole drawing nearer.

Sitting in my chair, in situ at home, a few bandages here and there where rocks must have grazed me. My foot...No, my foot is fine. There's nothing wrong with my foot. I don't feel like walking around, so I don't. I don't feel like using crutches—why would I need crutches? My foot is fine. My head is sore, my neck is so stiff I hardly dare move it, but I don't feel impaired in my thinking at all, and my foot doesn't hurt at all. So where does the gun come from? Was the gunsmoke really just a funny smell from the wreck? It's like I'm still smelling it.

Did Renbrui shoot somebody?

The birdhouse stands there like a tall torch, sooty black, still waiting to be set on fire. No birds come to it. It disseminates a black pollen of waiting, the mysterious power of readiness. The longer the wait, the more the power of waiting grows, but only up to a point. There's a moment of no return, when too much time has passed, and the waiting dissipates into a nameless state that isn't failure, since, in the end, there was no test. What happens to all that unused readiness? Does it erode with time, or does it just wink away when the moment to come has gone by without ever being present?

I wait to see if a bird will emerge from the birdhouse. It's flying through a sky that has a little dark aperture in it, the entrance to this sky, through the birdhouse door. That would make the door of the birdhouse the point where the two skies meet.

"What do you expect to see come out?" Daladara asked.

I suddenly feel very tired.

"I expect to see...I don't know," I say.

"Then why watch it?"

"I don't know. Maybe I'll get to see nothing."

"You mean, you're waiting to see..." and Daladara completes the sentence with a gesture, waving his two hands, opening them as if he were releasing something toward and away from the entirety of the world.

"Right," I say. "The thing I came to see."

"It shows you...It doesn't show you what it *is*..."

"I mean, it *does*, but..."

"Yeah, right, it *does*. You get shown a thing. But it's the showing that counts."

"You don't see it."

"No, you don't see it—I kind of get it, yeah. It's like, not a mirror, not showing you you or how you see or anything to do with yourself—"

"Nothing to do with me," I say with an assurance that I utterly don't feel.

"Like, it's not *about you*—?"

"Right."

"But it's...Aw *man!*"

"Yeah, see?"

"Yeah, right, OK."

He opens the back and puts in a couple of potted plants all bound up with fabric. I ask him what they are.

"White Lies..." he says.

He shuts the back and sits down beside me a moment later in the passenger's seat.

"It's a rose variety."

"Called 'white lies'?"

"Yup."

"I didn't know you had a garden."

"I just plant them where I think they should grow. I've got roses all over town."

I drop him off in Hollywood, near Los Feliz.

I'm finishing up my lunch when the magic charges me, like a boxer coming out of his corner at the bell. Striated lights, black and white, shimmer over the customers and the walls in geometric and symmetrical patterns. As I pay, get up, and head out through the patterns, four points of brilliant cold light appear on the sidewalk outside the door and emit snow white lasers that fold down against the ground delineating a pathway between two parallel beams.

Follow the path—not like I can avoid it—pumping my arms but I'm only walking, pant for breath, doing nonstop math unconsciously, my eyes lock onto the points where the lasers end, where they slice upward into the air and then pivot down to form the next leg, right down the sidewalk.

My face is so tense. I can see myself half transparent against an orange sky—no, the light is orange but the sky is blue—wearing the cold placenta of the sun on my head like a half-deflated shopping bag, pumping wiry fists, my eyes fixed on a spot where the sky is closer and going black. Where is she? Look down...bend down to see the skyscrapers of downtown Los Angeles protruding through my bare left foot, like so many blue glass nails. The buildings look solid, my foot looks solid, there's no injury, no pain, no blood: the lights and reflections from the buildings seep into my foot and discolor it. I stand up again, pushing my head and shoulders up through the clouds to the bright blue white sky around me, the distant half-dancing figures I only now recognize from earlier, when I was in the street, are replaced by shrouded persons whose attitudes are hidden from me, except to say that the magic hasn't finished. Where is she? What neighborhood? Maybe the beach?

I look around for whatever is supposed to come next and

find it on my hands, dazzling arterial red, welling up across each of my palms spelling BLACK on my left hand and BRANE on my right, the red turns clear and the letters ball up into two pairs of teardrops I raise to my eyes. The eerie cold as my eyes drink them. My pupils twist into auspicious knots. All this time there have been voices, and writing, but none of it matters. There's pain behind it. I can only know it through the voices, the writing, these obliques and oracular gibbering. The mottos written on the walls and streetsigns are all in an alphabet that looks like long ribbons of smoke, and the speech is indistinct, as if it were baffled inside a small, bare room.

It wasn't me, though. I was living a description of someone else's memories, so when other people inside that moment looked my way they didn't see me, they saw whoever it is who lived this. It was a memory without hindsight, so I didn't understand what was happening any better than whoever it is who lived this understood it when it happened to them. It's not one of *her* memories, I don't think. No, I'm sure it's not.

"What happened to you?"

"I had a run-in with some uh devotees," Daladara says.

"I was at the Mexican cafeteria on Los Feliz. I asked for the check. Then I notice my shoe's untied, which was weird because I only just tied it as I came in. I bend down to tie my shoe, and the check tray is there on the table when I sit up again. This was on top."

He hands me an enamel pin of a grouchy face wrapped in red cape. Only one of the two eyes has a pupil in it.

"It's Domo-kun, right?"

"Daruma."

"Oh yeah, damn."

"There was a little rolled up note stuck in the spikes on the back, with a where and a when printed on it, and come alone. It's the way they have of arranging meetings."

"You mean like unfinished business, or...?"

"Well or finishing something, more like."

"You couldn't say no?"

"I could, but they wouldn't have asked me so nicely the next time, and I wanted to know why they were interested in me. I just came from there."

His face clouds over a little.

"No...no I went home first. The meeting was...ah yesterday..."

He fumbles with a cigarette and lights it.

"Excuse me a second," he says, his voice muffled by smoke. After a few drags the light starts to rekindle in his eyes again.

"I guess they rocked me harder than I thought they did."

"What happened? Did they get violent...?"

"No, not exactly. They don't use regular violence. I'll tell you what happened. When I got there, the address turned out to be a straight-edge Mormon dance club. I was flagged the moment I stepped through the front door. Not a lot of black faces in there. A guy came right up to me, got in my ear, and said they were waiting for me in the back, and just to go through. So I walked across the dance floor, through all six people there, past the linebacker they had watching the rear, and into a room that was like techno Sunday school. White, clean, sterile, with some Ikea chairs and tables, empty. Only one door.

"After about five minutes, the linebacker came in and told me to sit down in a specific chair, back to the door. I told him I was happy standing up, and he said it wasn't a request, I could leave now, or I could sit down, and then he folded his veiny forearms at me. So, I sat down. I heard him leave. I'm sitting there, alone, as far as I could tell, boom boom boom going on. A big no smoking sign on the wall. Then they came in with a bang behind me."

"'Don't turn around!' One of them yells. He walks to where I can see him, along with four other guys. I started to smell chlorine when they come in; it was like they carried the smell with them, like cologne. I was supposed to think the guy who told me not to turn around was the leader. The other four were all kind of young-looking, clean cut, you know, not a hair out of place. They wore matching white outfits, white Japanese Shinto paper bracelets. The pretend leader was about their age. He had a white oversize Japanese streetwear type hoodie over a white turtleneck. They do this thing...they're not Japanese, they're not Shinto, they're not Mormons. They just mix and match."

"What do they call themselves?"

"I'm sure they have a groovy name, but I don't know it. Around outside trash like us, they just call themselves 'the little group.' The idea is that there's a special power that comes from using stuff like Daruma out of context, doing it wrong. So they probably have some kind of eclectic, random name, like a Tibetan name or something.

"Anyway, the fake leader sat down opposite me with both his hands on the table. Then he claps his hands once, and the guys behind him all do it, too. He pulls out a water bottle with the label off, takes a drink, and suddenly I'm thirsty. That's how they start. The other four guys are doing stuff behind me I'm not allowed to look at. I can hear them kind of moving around. The main guy is just staring at me. The thing is that they're dangerous and corny at the same time. They do a thing..."

For a moment a look of fright passes over his face. His mouth stalls in mid sentence and his lips tremble. Then he blinks it away. The furrows remain on his forehead until he passes his hand over them. Then his face relaxes.

"Yeah," he says then. "They have a way of..."

He sighs, breaks off.

"It's like you're dreaming. That feeling you get that you're dreaming when you know you're awake. And then it's like the world is breaking ice and you have to go, move, keep out of the cracks, but I had to sit there and watch the crack open up and break toward me. The fake leader's head was like a visual distortion where his head should be. It was sort of tan around the edges, like there was a wreath of tan clouds around a blob of oil that was like blue in the middle, with dull stars inside, like an old movie company logo in space, and the booming behind me just completely stopped. It was like my heart stopped. And those guys behind me kept moving, doing whatever they were doing, milling around, and I could feel their air on me, the chlorine smell. Then I hear a voice behind me, right down in the quiet, say:

"'You wouldn't be doing anything that'd fuck up our purity would you, Daladara?'

"Now that was the real boss. He'd come in after those others, in the silence.

"I said, 'What purity is that?'

"And they came back with anguish—like I had to bite back tears."

"Were they hitting you?"

"No no, this was the magic. They were leaning in, they were pressing and probing, looking for an opening. The voice went—

"'*Our* purity, Daladara. You've been busy fucking with the world lately and the brothers and I want some assurances from you that you aren't doing anything that we need concern ourselves about. Right, brothers?'

"And then they really poured it on. When that happens, you have to dummy up because anything you say will give away too much, but you have to say fuck you, eat shit, you're just a dainty little bunch of weebs, anything defiant to keep the cracks from, you know, going inside. When they saw I wasn't going to give them anything that way, they eased it back to a dull searing.

"'We can get along fine, Daladara. Just a little cooperation, some mutual respect, Daladara.'

"All of sudden, I can hear the four guys leave. I think the real boss left too, although not entirely. He was still tuned in, even if wasn't physically there. I was left with that fake boss, and he told me there were certain places and people I should avoid if I didn't want to get a visit."

"What did they mean by their 'purity'?"

"It's their main thing; they try to generate and proliferate this exclusivity field they call purity. They do salt drawings in hidden spots and leave paper amulets and ropes and stuff in specific locations tied to a magnetic oracle some way. They're mostly in the Valley but they have their special domains outside as well. So, once he's done laying out the details, the real guy comes up right behind me and says,

"'Daladara, perhaps we can be friends.'

"'I love friends.'

"He pats me on the shoulder, once for each word."

"'Friends...help...friends...'

"His hands were super-staticky and they give me these microshocks. I don't answer and he says:

"'Is there some way we could help you, Daladara?'

"I'm thinking—you could go fuck yourself, that's how you could help me, but I say 'I can't think of any' and he says

"'Let us know if you do, won't you, Daladara?'

"I say, 'Can do.'"

"Then a map of LA county drops down into my lap, unfolded, and my hands just jump out, snatch and grab at it. There are whole neighborhoods that are surrounded by a heavy white border and scribbled in. And the voice says—

"'The white zones—nothing racial in the term, you understand—'

"I say, 'Naturally.'

"'Some of our best friends,' he says.

"'Uh-huh, I got it,' I say.

"'And then there's always—you, Daladara,' he says.

"'Always,' I say. He gave my shoulder a squeeze there when he said it, and I got another bad feeling, like my heart was suddenly full of air, like sickroom air.

"'The white zones are off limits, for your safety's sake,' he says.

"I say, 'Nice of you think of me.'

"Right on cue, he says, 'We think of everything, Daladara.'"

"His hand was gone. He was gone. I was alone, but they left me the map."

Daladara pulls a triple A map out of his back pocket and

shows it to me. He points to barely visible writing in white colored pencil at the bottom—"if you need something call," and then a phone number.

"So you've been warned, then" I say lamely.

"I have been warned," he says. "I have always been warned. I was born warned. I was always going to be someone who just stopped showing up one day."

"So you're going to just vanish?"

"Definitely," he says.

He looks out at the grounds, toward the mountains, diaphanous as stone.

"But I'll never stop coming back."

I notice a rose bush there along his eyeline, nestled among the shrubs in a planter over by the benches, separated from the lawn by a low barrier of rocks all painted white.

"Until I do."

I'll write about Daladara's secret life, Renbrui's secret life. I refuse to say a word about my life. I work hard to cultivate a faculty for engrossing myself in other people's stories as much as I am in my own story. More. I will not dignify what has happened to me by turning it into a story. I'll defer to them, the real characters.

Parking was tough that day and I'd had to find a spot on the far side of campus. I came in through some unfamiliar buildings, finding my way uncertainly from point to point, navigating largely by keeping the distant mountains on my right. I'm passing the gym, and I see her there, on the exercise bicycle nearest the tinted glass wall. She doesn't see me. Her eyes are staring at some spot in the distance, out across the quad, as if everything she loved, or hated, were concentrated there. Her face and her exposed forearms are beet red, sweat drips from her nose and chin. The pedals spin beneath her feet with a leaden smoothness that suggests to me that she's turned the difficulty up high and she's pushing a lot of weight. I feel too self-conscious to walk past her; I don't like her to think I'm watching her, so I reverse my steps, take a longer route around one of the buildings, still imagining her there, churning those heavy wheels, glaring through a mask of sweat, through space, at something in her mind.

Suddenly, I'm reminded of a time when she passed me in the hall, hurrying on with her clipboard to some other task, and a slip of paper escaped, unnoticed, from the sheaf of documents she was always carrying. It fluttered to the ground, over by the wall. My first impulse was to draw her attention to it, but curiosity got the better of me, I guess. I suspect I was thinking that finding the paper gave me a pretext to seek her out and see her again, that telling her, then and there, that I'd found it, meant squandering a chance to bother her later.

I examined it, of course. She'd covered one side with double-digit numbers and added them all together, then divided them by a decimal. The reverse side had these words written on it, also in her handwriting:

no soul no feelings only work—fragrant thread

Those words came back to me when I thought of her grinding rigidly away on the bicycle, and it struck me that her unwavering gaze had been a beam projecting her soul and feelings out of herself, driving them away with persistent, exhausting physical activity.

TIME
what is it
grow up grow old
I don't know anything, not alone or together, not
anything or nothing. Don't grow up old.

Dr. Shitansky was conferring with a large pot-bellied man in a tailored Nehru tunic, all black and tightly buttoned. This man had pulled his chair around to her side of the desk, so that she would have to speak to him by leaning to one side while he listened impassively without looking at her. Every now and then he will comment, leaning a little toward her, his hands laced over his gut. He has a wide loose-lipped mouth that ripples and curls over his closed teeth when he speaks, like a curtain in a breeze. I'd seen him around the Institute from time to time and I remembered then that Renbrui had pointed him out to me as Dr. Shitansky's attorney. There's a sinisterly un-Californian air about him; he's like a villainous advisor.

As I came back after lunch, I caught sight of Dr. Shitansky's attorney sitting on one of the benches, hands splayed over his broad black twill knees, with a huge meerschaum pipe clamped in his jaw. His lips seemed to collect the smoke from each puff, convey them across to the other side of his face, and then release them into the air. The smoke had a penetrating, cloyingly sweet aroma.

I was talking with Allegre. He tells me he absolutely has to get the something or other working or something something about electricity and fire, so I have to follow him. Can he just tell me the numbers to fill in the form with no he can't he has to get readings from whatever it is. So we go down to the fucking thing, and he works on it and works on it while I wait, and he finally finishes, and then he can fill in the forms, putting the numbers in the boxes and smearing grease and machine snot all over the paper as well. Then we're suddenly both too jaded to move or do much more than sit and stare.

"I used to have a golden retriever named Wally," he said to me randomly. "So, once, we were taking a walk. There was this high ridge line and we liked to walk along the top of it. You could see everything from up there. So we're walking like we've done a million times before, and Wally takes and leaves the path to go look at something in the high grass, and then he's gone. I can't see him because the grass is high. So I run over and I see him just as he kind of launches off the slope, trying to jump back or I don't know. It looked funny for just that second, but then he fell and landed way down there. I remember feeling a blast of cold that went all through me. I'll never forget how that felt. I could see him lying on his side down on a sort of outcrop. His eye was open. I didn't even think about it. I just ran down the slope for him. I kept saying no, no the whole way down.

"He was already gone when I reached him. It didn't make sense, his being gone that fast. I didn't know what to do with him. I felt betrayed. It was like the day had tricked me into trusting it. And then it did that to me."

Tears welled in his eyes.

"It killed my friend."

He blinked, and sniffed violently. I didn't want to embarrass him by handing him a tissue but I did it anyway and he took it and blew his nose.

"He died because he trusted me when I said it was a regular day. But that was because I trusted that day. I couldn't get up and just leave—leave him. I couldn't do anything. Everything was just like—Wally's dead. Just like that. From everything, for no reason, with no mistakes. I didn't do anything wrong."

All I remember of the dream is coming into a room thinking Renbrui was there then, and maybe I might catch a glimpse of her...That is, I think I saw her for a second...THAT IS, I was looking around when I heard something or noticed something, and, as I was turning my eyes to that thing, whatever it was, I thought I caught a glimpse of Renbrui in that room...but somehow my eyes didn't stop turning toward the distracting thing until they'd found it, by which time they'd forgotten what they were looking for, and the distraction had forgotten how to go on being there, so, even if I was looking right at whatever it was that distracted me, I was thinking about nothing but Renbui and didn't even know what to look for or why I was looking, and then I looked back and Renbrui of course wasn't in the room or anywhere, or was no longer there.

Of course I had to go into the room and look, and where she had been standing, I guess, assuming I actually had seen her in the room at all, there was a tarot card on the floor. I can only remember that it was all in shades of blue, that it had two figures on it, two crowned figures, and they were sort of dancing or grappling in front of a starry sky, maybe in a garden or on a palace wall. The figure on the right was a little lower than the one on the left, an ibis-headed king, the simple, jagged crown hovering above its head. Floating draperies...elegant hands... that's all I remember.

"This desire is your enemy," says a voice, familiar from my past. It's always been there to shore me up, it seems, with archaically stern admonitions like this one. It's trying to steer me away from a repetition of past humiliations, as if it were my Calvinist duty not to embarrass myself by succumbing to the blandishments of a beautiful dream. In my mind's eye, Renbrui looms over me smiling. Since her eyes are completely hidden by her fringe, I have no way of knowing whether she is smiling at me and, from this angle, I can't be too sure that she isn't really sneering anyway.

I'm listening to music in my headphones, rocking back and forth a little. There's a little folder of old photos lying open in front of me, and the reflections of the light catch on the rumpled surface of the plastic. As I move to and fro, the reflections swell and diminish, hollowing out as they expand into warped hoops and then filling in again as they shrink. It would be terrifying if that were happening while I sat without moving. Just those blobs of light opening and closing like little mouths. It wouldn't take anything more than that to make me question my sanity, would it? Photos of...

I have to keep telling their stories. Every time there's a pause, my own story starts to demand my attention again, and that's the last thing I want. I have to fill up my time with their stories if I don't want to be caught alone with mine. I don't cry over tragedies; I cry when I reflect. I imagine Allegre reunited with his dead dog in paradise, the two of them gazing at each other, restored to each other, suffused with each other, so they can never love each other enough. I don't think there's anyone waiting for me there, not that way, and if there is, I don't know that it matters that much to me, although I know that it should, and that my indifference, if that's what it is, is a sign that there's something brutally damaged inside, and that induces me to live in perennial leavetaking. I hope I'm wrong. I always am, so that's not unlikely. In heaven, the suffering face of the spirit who can't contain the intensity of its joy, surrounded by the angels, impassive, neutral, absently benign, angels, a happiness so fierce it is as wild as anguish and as impossible to bear.

I'm back at my desk when suddenly I realize I'm not alone. I look up, and there's Dr. Corngholm standing there, thrusting a bundle of neatly wrapped and labelled papers at me.

"For you to archive up," he says.

He bounces away.

As part of "archiving up" a document, I have to prepare a summary of it derived from its *precis*. In this case, the papers are a typewritten report labelled

OBSERVATIONS OF SEMEOPHERIC VACUA

MAP REF. 34° 8' 33.0324" N / 118° 15' 18.2664" W

5/1/30 to 5/7/30

and there is no *precis* included. So I can wait for the next blue moon to catch Dr. Corngholm again long enough to ask him for a *precis*, or I can try to come up with a summary myself and get this thing finished now. Luckily the bulk of it is charts.

Dr. Corngholm is evidently using a surprisingly extensive network of volunteer linguistic spotters to track the use of words in electronic communications originating in, or destined for, specific areas on the map. He refers to something he calls "the semeosphere," which is I guess something like the atmosphere for words, and he's looking for sudden drops in the frequency with which a given word may occur. He instructs his spotters to pay special attention to any messages involving what he calls "injunctions to memory." From the samples he provides, I take it that he wants them to flag any message in which someone is urging someone else to remember something, taking this as an index of a "potential lapse point." I guess they mail him the results, or hand them in to him personally, so that he can maintain Dr. Shitansky's internet cordon.

I flip through his charts. Just curious. It turns out that, for the designated period, and in the designated area, the word "black" seems to have disappeared entirely from the lexicon of messages. Dr. Corngholm notes that, while he doesn't have any control data for this particular location respecting this particular word, his "lexical frequency index" for the "greater Los Angeles area" indicates that the word "black" typically falls into his "common" category, second only to "ubiquitous" words like "the," "and," "like," "yes," and so on, in probable occurrence. There's a chart that specifies how likelihood is determined and what the various thresholds are for his categories.

I ask Daladara if this area corresponds to the white zone he told me about, and he says no.

"What's the one word you can't say in the white zone?" he asks.

"Black? But that's not in the white zone."

"I'm not saying it is. I'm telling you how it works."

"So it's white?"

"It's white. You can't say white in the white zone, because every word you say within the white zone, at least if you're one of the ones establishing and persisting it, is a white word. So, if you say 'white' in the white zone, you cancel it, right? If you have to say white while you're in the white zone, then you're saying that you have to say white, when, if the white zone is really there and functioning, everything you say is supposed to be automatically white."

"Like you're not maintaining it, or you're questioning it?"

"Right."

"Then this area would be a black zone?"

"Right."

"So who made that?"

"I don't know. It wasn't me."

"Could it be a by-product of creating a white zone? Like all the black gets chased out of the white zone and collects over here?"

"Could be. Couldn't say why there, though. Or why it wouldn't just disperse evenly."

The PA crackles and we are eagerly invited to a pop meeting in the auditorium. Dr. Shitansky is red faced and almost hyperventilating, Dr. Liu beams, seems as though she is about to burst into song. Dr. Corngolm sits with his legs spread, hands on knees, grinning from ear to ear. Dr. Shitansky has studied his report.

"Everyone, everyone!" Dr. Shitansky says ecstatically, brandishing the pages, "We have a lead on an entangled particle!"

Dr. Shitansky believes that Dr. Corngolm's linguistic black hole is an indication that a particle entangled with a physical black hole is somewhere in that area, and sucking up every instance of the word "black" in every language present. At a later, much calmer, meeting, we are told in laborious detail about the mathematical-geographical procedure by means of which the likely position of the entangled particle was calculated.

"We've determined that the particle is almost certainly in this structure."

Dr. Liu, standing by the overhead projector, describes a circle with her pointer around a building in the center of the transparency. It's an overhead photograph of a neighborhood up in the foothills, where the houses are tucked up against the ridge lines. From above, this particular building looks like three drab white rectangles staggered and joined to form one ragged outline. I immediately recognize it as one of those small apartment buildings you find inserted seemingly at random among single-occupancy houses in Los Angeles county.

"We went down in person to the housing records archive and found out that there's a bomb shelter on the property. I don't think you can see it even in person, let alone in this photo, but there's no record of its ever having been taken out," Allegre says.

"We think the particle is in there," Dr. Liu says.

"Lights!" Dr. Shitansky says.

Renbrui snaps the switch and the fluorescents blink on with dull, soft chiming.

"Thank you, Dr. Liu and Engineer Allegre," she drones. "Now the task at hand is to extract the particle from that location and transmit it here to the Institute for study. We have developed a plan, and the purpose of this meeting is to explain that plan, to ensure that we all grasp it with maximum clarity. If we are not meticulously precise in our execution of this plan, we could lose this particle forever, and we can't practicably study it *in situ*."

She scans the room, moving her eyes but not her head. I recognize this posture—it's the same one she adopts when she's undergoing the experiments. This room-scan very pointedly includes me. It even lingers on me. What does that mean?

"Every one of you will have a role to play," she says, eyes still on me. "Dr. Liu and Engineer Allegre will be operating the transmission equipment here. I will be undergoing an experiment at the time of transmission in order to see if there's any special hole-related incident associated with it, and Renbrui will supervise. Given the location of the house, Mr. Daladara will take certain measures to ensure that we will not be interfered with by any outsiders. Mr. Gross will be the one we send to the property to acquire the particle."

"You'd better not fuck this up, Gross," Renbrui says from her station by the door.

"No one is going to fuck anything up, Renbrui!" Dr. Shitansky says sharply. "I will brief Mr. Gross personally."

"I'm not an idiot," I say.

"No one is calling you one, Mr. Gross," Dr. Shitansky says in a tone of command.

She rises from her seat, stepping over Bas, and picks up a hideous light blue backpack. Setting it on the table we've set up by the overhead projector, she pulls four metal boxes out of it and sets them down in a row. Then she draws out a brown plastic compass, a brass theodolite, and a sort of black flashlight, and puts them down next to the boxes.

"Now, these boxes are all you need to establish the transmission. Each box will be set up at one of the four cardinal points around the property."

She points to the all but invisible image still projected on the wall. Then she indicates the compass and other gear.

"You will use this equipment to position the transmitters at the correct distances from each other. Once you find your spot—
"

She picks up one of the boxes in both hands, clumsily turning it this way and that while she acts out what I am supposed to do.

"—you extend these four legs on the bottom, extend the antenna, point it toward the Institute, encircle the device on the ground with this attached chain, and flip this switch. Then you leave it and go on to the next one. This one—"

She plants a finger firmly on the last box in the row, which is indistinguishable from the others.

"Is the one you place last. When you flip its switch, we will receive a signal back here, telling us that the circuit is complete. If the circuit is not complete, that means one or more of the boxes is not in the right place. If that happens, the light here—"

She shows me the light.

"—will not light up. In that case, you'll have to go back and verify the respective positions of the boxes and make whatever adjustments may be necessary, then check to see if the light is still on. If the light is off—no, scratch that, I mean on, if the light is on, then you can go. Just leave the boxes where they are."

Daladara pulls me over, looks me straight in the eye and says —"If anything really strange starts to happen to you while you're out there, say ZAMAN WISLIN in your mind."

He leaves before I can answer.

I have to pass through the "white zone," going both there and back. My destination is on the other side, up in the hills. All the way there I'm rehearsing my palaver in case I get caught or questioned.

"Well you see—I represent—work for—I'm here from…I'm here surveying for the Temporary Institu—I'm surveying this neighborhood for the Institute for the Study of Holes."

That's when I would flash my ID, if I had an ID.

Jack Webb voice: "What holes, ma'am? Subterranean holes, deep under the earth. Sort of like fault lines, sinkholes, and potential sinkholes."

The map is open, folded awkwardly and taped to the dashboard, my route marked out in pink highlighter. No computers. Into the foothills, below the otherworldly San Gabriel mountains. Off the highway and down empty streets lined with suburban homes like adobe missions, ranches, pagodas, Tudor houses. The road angles up, and the building swims out of the background, swaying with the car as I manage the turns. As arranged, I park on the turn off by a gated trail head, where a tawny dirt path straggles toward a concrete fire trench and the upper ridge line. It's a bright day, and hot. My face is already sore from squinting through the windshield.

Quiet up here. No wind. No clouds. The sky is deep, mineral blue. Right overhead, it's all but blue-black. I have the feeling I stick out conspicuously from the planet's surface. I sling grotesque backpack on and start looking around self-consciously for the landmarks that should help me to identify roughly where to go. It's all very unreal, like the arbitrary tasks in an improvised children's game, where certain activation properties are assigned to objects in a field like kind of overlay.

The first landmark, a wooden sign painted brown with white letters cut into it, I find right away on the corner. It says: UPPER EMERALD ISLE PARK. Beyond it, a tiny public meadow with two stone chess tables and a playground consisting of one battered swing set and a three-seater merry-go-round standing at a tilt in a plot of sand. The trees here are low but spreading, roofing over the park and giving it a cavernous quality. I stand in the spongy, crumbled-bark ground cover spread around the sign, fumbling in the backpack. I align the compass and then read the theodolite, figuring the exact spot. Around me, nothing but sunlight direct from space, silent suburban houses, the empty miniature park with its amenities all standing idle, and sparse bird song. Once I've checked my work and returned twice to the same spot, I plant the first box there, laying the ball-bearing chain around it and switching it on. Hope no one messes with it.

Now for number two I will have to go over to the far side of the target building, and only now do I look at it directly. It's built like four white shoeboxes set side by side, staggered and canted to form a saw-edge, slathered in glittering white stucco, a grey-green asterisk star thing bolted onto the front. It's the sort of place that looks like it should have a visible name, like "The Malibu" or "Vista del Monte," in elegant cut metal lettering across the front. Each box has its own garage door, not quite facing the street, and there's a single entrance all the way over on the right—a gate painted green, but now faded to a bilious, all but grey color. The place stands out incongruously, the one apartment building among all these houses, and I find it hard to imagine just who would live there or how. Then again, why not?

I feel more discreet walking up the sidewalk opposite. I cross, and ascend the narrow way bordering the property. This street angles sharply up toward the ridgeline. From my rising vantage point, I can see no signs of life. Every window is curtained off. No lights, no sound.

The street ends, rounding off in a continuous curve below what little is left of the slope, dotted with old oak trees, and the sky beyond. As I reach for my compass, I see a white-haired old lady in the back of the property, in a blue mumu and flip flops, watering the concrete. Why do they do that? I can just as readily imagine her, lost in a senile haze, watering a garden that isn't there, as I can imagine that she has her reasons, drawn from old-world California wisdom. Maybe wet concrete doesn't crack in the heat? I guess it's reassuring that the place isn't completely deserted. I don't know why that thought should be reassuring. It would only make sense to be reassured if the place were abandoned, so I wouldn't have to worry about hassling anyone or getting hassled back. So, my emotion is rationally unjustified. I'm glad I was able to get that cleared up. It should help a lot.

I get the second box placed, again taking my time, checking my work, feeling foolish. If anyone sees me and gets nosy, it's better that I work in an unhurried way, without any haste or furtiveness. I needn't worry, though—there's no one here. Just the occasional bird squeal, not even a breath of wind. There's a dull, metallic thudding coming from the property somewhere, a listless noise, like a piece of something dangling, knocking now and again on something else. With no wind, what's making it swing, I wonder?

The woman has gone inside. The concrete back yard is now all water-bronzed and scintillating in the glare. I head up to the top and take in the sprawling city below me, vibrating and ablaze with daylight, completely silent. The landmark for the third box position is an especially large live oak, over toward the south and up high. I get set up there, no problems. No big deal, like any trivial chore.

The last box is the trickiest. It goes on the west corner, and to get there I have to drive down the slope and through all the tough, leathery brush, until I reach a little jumble of boulders, then pace off twelve feet by the compass and some more rigamarole. The real concern is that this puts me technically on the property, which means trespassing. Crashing through the bracken isn't going to be quiet, either, or quick—anyone in the building who might be glancing outside would see me, and probably hear me. I fully expect to be accosted. Maybe by that old lady.

I head down the slope, my arms up and folded in front of me, protecting my face as I drive through the chaparal. All the plants are stiff, thorny, clingy, a little poisonous maybe. They lash and snatch at me as I drive my body forward into them. I emerge covered in spikes, toxic wax, little pinlike seeds, forty different kinds of irritating pollen. With the white stucco outline hovering over me, I measure the distances, take readings, and set up the box. When I flip the switch on box four, the little light goes on and I sigh with relief. I won't have to go back and reposition any of them. I don't know what to do, though, about that light—won't it attract attention after dark? But it will be all done with its work by the time night falls.

As I wonder about this, I find myself listening to something. A cricket. It's not time for crickets, but I hear one, just one. The sound echoes strangely. I listen to it. A listless chirping, as if the cricket were asleep, sleep-chirping. It's coming from inside the building. The dull, metallic thudding sounds again, too. And just then I decide it's time to go. The street is right there, but I'd have to climb a fence and push up and over a little rise that's thicketed in more thorny desert plants, dense as a cultivated hedge. Doubling back is less trouble. I climb up to the ridge top again, leaning forward, nearly bent double, panting, breathing dust, making broad swimming motions with my arms, latching on gingerly to crumbling rocks and brittle branches. The foliage presses me back. I really have to work just to stay where I am, let alone move forward. Redolent of bruised leaves and smelling like a basket of dried herbs, I finally disengage and stumble back toward the nice even asphalt, my feet crunching in shoes filled with grit and miscellaneous sharp natural objects. I pass box three, and then box two. My nose is stopped with dust, and I blink grains of sand from my eyes, not daring to touch my face with these ripped, stinging fingers.

I'm about a third of the way back down the side street when the ground swivels abruptly beneath my feet. My attention, my thoughts, all my sense impressions contract to a single point somewhere inside me and I freeze, aware of a low, subsiding rumble, a total suspension of bird song and other noise.

By the time I can think about what to do, the tremor has already passed, leaving an aura of vacancy behind. Everything resets. The moment the tremor hit, I looked up—just another startled animal—but I heard the dull, metallic thudding, the chirps of that cricket recirculate off the walls somewhere inside the building, and I saw the old woman in the back yard. I watch the water pouring out of the limp hose and splattering the bone-dry concrete slabs of the paved back yard. I recognize the water. It's the same water, catching the same daylight. The daylight of empty afternoons. The blankness of nothing, of happening again without having happened, without being able to happen again.

"Trapped—you're trapped—you're stuck...forever—"

I hear the dull metallic thudding, the muffled and echoing cricket chirping listlessly. I see the water fall from the drooping hose and darken the grey-white concrete in jagged shapes, like dark rents torn in light fabric. The ground rolls beneath my feet.

"Trapped—you're trapped..."

The old woman is turning on the hose, darkness spreads around it where it lies coiled up baking in the sun. She goes over to it and picks up one end, bending carefully. Then she shuffles forward into the yard, holding the hose two feet up from the gushing end. There's a dull, metallic thudding somewhere, a cricket...

"Trapped..."

The earth beneath me yaws just a bit, I nearly stumble, throw out an arm, lean back along the slope. There's the old lady from before, unperturbed, shuffling out from the apartment building and heading for a green garden hose lying coiled in the sun. Water slaps the ground, drops from the hose in a folding, thick rope of chaotic spurting. The old lady turns her whole body this way and that to spread it around on the dry concrete paving over the—

The world rolls from beneath my feet. No light.

"There's nothing but you."

Total loss.

"Just you, forever and ever."

Bottomless grief, losing and losing and losing...dwindling... smaller and smaller...lesser and lesser...

I'm sitting in my car, hands on the wheel. The backpack is on the passenger seat. The sun is blazing in through the windshield. I'm reading the wooden park sign over and over again without understanding it. My eyes smart. My face is sore, lined with salt, and my throat burns as if I'd been screaming. I don't remember coming down, getting in the car. That's time lost down the hole.

It's raining outside. I can hear it. Although I know this room has at least one outside wall, the rain seems to be falling somewhere far from me, down long, door-lined hallways. This pain isn't me. I look down in despair at my withered arms and legs, my flabby, useless body. I was never a particularly strong person, but it seems as if I've lost an incredible amount of strength, more than I ever had. I want to hack off my legs and get free of them, but the poison is in my mind, the poison of rain, and silence, isolation, weakness, tedium.

I know what's in my mind. That day, it happened. That was the moment, when I was looking at the old lady with her hose, her wet concrete backyard, hearing the thudding, the cricket, and the gear I'd set up performed its function.

This is my great secret, the one I am depending on to account for everything, so it had better. Dr. Liu explained that quantum entanglement could propagate itself to additional particles under the right circumstances. The circumstances on that day, at that place and time, caused the particle in the building to propagate its entanglement to another one that just happened to be *part of the structure of my own brain*. This means that there is, right now, a particle *in my brain* that is entangled with a particle currently inside the event horizon of black hole NGC 1313 X-2. There are three entangled particles.

One in a black brane, one in a building or a property in the Los Angeles foothills, and one in my own brain.

This should mean nothing more than that measuring the spin of the particle in my brain would affect the spin of those other particles. That's all entanglement involves, as far as I know—the determination of spin for particle A here on earth will result in a separate but precisely simultaneous determination of spin for particle B out there, and, I guess, for my own particle C. Since no one has measured the spin of any of these particles, none of them can have been determined yet. But I am telling you: I have a particle in my brain that is entangled with a particle inside a black hole, a particle that is always looking directly down into the heart of black hole into which it is falling. It is outside and inside, watching itself fall—forever.

In a dizzying wave of fear I wonder if I've had a stroke, or some other kind of serious medical episode. I touch my forehead, my face, the crown of my head, feeling for the problem. I tell myself I have to get to an emergency room. But, as I pull out into the street, into a u-turn, and begin rolling back down out of the hills, I lose that feeling. Everything around me is regular, boring, and so am I. The day's been a little weird, that's all. Just weird. The thought of the old lady watering the concrete returns, my breath catches in my chest and I nearly slam on the brakes.

OK, so we don't think about that.

About what?

Exactly. An unrelated incident. An isolated episode...

TISH seems deserted when I get back, but in the end I find them all in the auditorium, bathed in summer light, gathered around Dr. Shitansky, like apostles around the savior. She's sitting in the experimental chair, the sheet of metal with the hole in it is suspended about a foot above her head, her face gleaming with perspiration as she turns to me, eyes shining.

"You did it, Gross!" she says.

Even Renbrui looks pleased, in a wild-eyed way.

It's all a dream. I'm still in the street, which has only just swayed and trembled beneath me. Instinctively, I stare at my own feet, as if they had something important to convey to me, and now that the danger seems passed, I'm looking up, seeing the woman watering concrete, and raising my eyes still further to meet the gaze falling from the window on the upper storey, where the heavy curtains stand parted.

Dazzling rays of sunshine crashing overhead make the darkness of the hooded window, beneath a short, arched awning of concrete, even deeper. The glass must be clear, but it looks smoked. The curtains float on the other side of the fixed pane running from floor to ceiling, dim in the gloom like specimens preserved in bottles of discolored preservative fluid, brown as tea. There was someone in that room, and they saw me through that window, from out of that dark panel. That was the moment I was entangled, I know it.

<hr>

The cricket chirps and I've lost it—whatever "it" was. Another dream, I guess. All I can remember is that I was standing in a dark room, a dark place, near one wall covered in burnt-out, mushroom-shaped light bulbs. A vertical field of faint crescent reflections.

I decide to find out where that cricket is and get out of bed, go through the door, pass down the empty hallway. I know it isn't night time. It's day time, but the daylight doesn't get inside. I keep trying to find my way to some place, only to discover that I'm already there every time, that this is it. The journey's end, directly underfoot from the start, all within reach without effort, not worth reaching for, not worth thinking about, and there wasn't any journey then.

I see Renbrui on the far side of the pond, ticking at her clipboard. More of the dream. All in white lace that elongates her and makes her seem lissome and ethereal. She's got goggles on, made of a strip of embroidered fabric. I've never seen her in those before, but somehow I know that she's compelled to wear them as a calmative. Along with the lace, the dimness of the garden under the heavy canopy of the late summer trees, the agitation of the water in the pool, the goggles give her a tragic aspect, like someone who's been blinded in a play. She walks slowly, her skirts trail on the ground, absorbed in book-keeping. Her face is composed and neutral, but I suspect she knows I'm here, gazing at her feverishly. As she goes, she passes in and out of deep shadows. The garden is decorated with sombre urns and vitrified ivy and crumbling Apollos and recondite nymphs and decapitated pans and phony pagodas that glow like sullen embers in the romantic gloom, and then Renbrui's profile flashes silhouetted against a peach and pink sky, framed in black boughs, entirely by chance. I think what I want to do is to sit, brimming with melancholy, at her feet as she stands there, listening to the nib of her ballpoint scratch its way over documents that crackle and groan as she wraps them over the top of the clipboard and continues her accounting on the next sheet. I glance up and her eyes are invisible behind two panes of glass that reflect the peach and pink sky. Her mouth crumples and her brows contract; she snaps her fingers at me.

"Eraser."

I slap my pockets but I've got nothing on me. Back into the house—maybe there...I can barely see the building. A grotesque outline in pale brown stone, with tall french windows, greenish tile inside, a single cricket chirping somewhere, and branching hallways. I turn into a room that might be mine; there's something familiar about it, but it's not oriented the way mine is. No, my room is behind us, with its back right up against the back of the world, while this room is pivoted ninety degrees. As long as it isn't a kitchen. Or the bathroom. With a figure slumped in the bath—

It's sideways as I come in, but deep and straight on, once I am in. Like a dining hall, long and high ceilinged. Windows way off on both sides and covered in ponderous curtains. The furni-ture might be wrecked or burned or maybe just covered with drop cloths. I guess I'm looking for a desk, a likely source of erasers. I'm under orders from a lady.

No desk. I find a cupboard ajar on a sort of bookshelf console sideboard thing, or china shelves, against the wall. Something is stirring in the cupboard. I draw the door open and a face comes floating out and grows until it occludes everything else in the dream. It's an expression of pain on a woman's face, and a man's face, an elderly face, a child's face, a baby's face, a middle-aged face, and passing through all the colors of skin and eyes, every human face that's ever been or ever will be, including mine, wracked with every kind of pain, wild-eyed, imploring it to stop.

The cataract of sunshine pouring down on TISH only makes the shadowy hallways darker, glassier, more cool, more dry. Motionless, overstimulated foliage on the outside of the glass shrieks and screeches, the light blazing off the leaves. I glance down at my blank memo pad, glance up again, and Renbrui is framed there in the middle of the hall before me like an epiphany; there's nowhere she could have come from, I don't know how she got there. She sweeps toward and around me with a fixed smile showing her little creepy white teeth, stately as a figurehead on the prow of a ship, her hair flowing down over the band that holds her goggle-lenses in place. Not a word or acknowledgement to me, but, once she's gone in a waft of her very light scent, there's an envelope on my desk that wasn't there before. It's blank. An ominous, sharp-edged panel of white. I don't want to tear it open for fear of offending it. I use the letter opener that came with the desk, made of pink plastic with a handle molded into the image of a Fuller brush man.

Inside, I find an official form, filled out by Dr. Shitansky, transferring directly to herself the supervision of the cleaners. I am to put up notices reminding them that all refuse, "down to the least particle of dust," must be submitted for gleaning to Dr.

Shitansky. While the notifications don't go into any details, I know the intention is to ensure that the particle we transferred from that building in the hillside, thanks to me, isn't inadvertently collected and discarded. While we know the particle is now here, physically at TISH, or in TISH, it hasn't yet been located. All anybody knows is that the particle is in here somewhere, maybe wedged in a brick, a window, a toilet bowl, or perhaps it tosses and turns, goes to and fro and up and down. The point is, that it might be lodged in something disposable, so we have to make sure we don't dispose of it. Allegre has come up with something that will determine whether or not the particle leaves the vicinity; it's a sort of scale that will light up the alert sign if the mass of the Institute is ever reduced by a specific quantity corresponding to the mass of the particle. I guess the particle in my brain has a different mass, since the alert never goes off when I leave.

Everyone here is expected to join in the search for the particle. "Locating the particle is our *maximum task* now," as Dr. Shitansky said. "The imperative to locate the particle is *at maximum*."

The particle in my brain forbids me to mention it to them, but, assuming it could be as useful for the project as the transmitted one, I wouldn't willingly discuss it anyway. I don't want my head in clamps. The black brane particle doesn't say anything to me, but it does mean things for me.

"Never let anything out," it means.

I think it selected me because I have a personal affinity with it along those lines. I give off nothing. I let nothing out. That's my apostolic vocation and the invisible black mass that drives ahead of me whenever I go, maintaining the distance between me and whatever comes up. Now that I can't move, or not without pain and reluctance and hesitation and uncertainty and planning and concentration and failure and replanning, everything recedes from me as my mind reaches for it, plummeting back in all directions, keeping its distance but not letting me go, holding me in blank, or, apostolically speaking, centered in my halo.

"Let it in."

Let what in?

"Death."

No!

"Let death in."

No!

Who's talking?

No!

Dr. Corngholm has written up a couple of questions that we are all supposed to ask ourselves at random intervals, and whenever we move from one room to another inside TISH. You can ask:

"What isn't remembering?"

or

"What do we call not being able to recall?"

And I think there were some other variants. The answer always involves forgetting. If we ask ourselves one of these questions and can't come up with answer, then we're supposed to contact Dr. Shitansky immediately, using a special emergency code number, 301745 (that's the number of characters in this MS so far, up to and including the last digit itself). You stay put, and then that everybody else is supposed to come and file through the same area, to see if they can't remember forgetting either, in the hope that this will be an indication of the proximity of the particle we're looking for. So far no one has called in the code. We all were given a pale green laminated card with the questions and the code neatly typed on it—guess who did the typing and the laminating.

I'm glad I'm not responsible for the fucking custodians any more. They never know what they're doing; they're like children. I'd be telling about a bone-dry dead toilet in one of the bathrooms and they'd be garlanding me with toilet paper, snickering behind their hands, getting into swatting matches with toilet brushes and plungers, wearing buckets on their heads like helmets, pushing themselves around in the wheeled trash bins like soap box racers. They were always injuring themselves somehow, but never from their horseplay; it was like they went home at night and really thought about new ways to screw up their work. They were always bandaged someplace, their hands and faces gouged and scarred. But when Dr. Shitansky talks, they listen like choirboys, heads down, eyes looking up at her. When she tells them to get something done, it gets done. It's as if their efficiency were indexed to the amount of respect their supervisor can get them to manifest.

———

Wake up, and it's as if my left ankle has somehow broken itself while I was asleep. A voice growls and whimpers in the room with me, I know it's mine. My hands keep flying up to hide my face. Nothing visibly wrong in the dim, dayless light in here with me; my foot isn't even red or swollen. It's just pain, by itself and for no reason, latching on to me at will.

Across the room I see an old woman withdrawing, pulling the door to as she goes. The look of compassion on her face, veiled in shadow, doesn't quite reach me. It loses itself in the intricate air of the room, on its way across the floor to the bed, and only its phantom can find me, at the bottom of a pit of meaningless wretchedness. I can smell my bitterly stale body that suffering has poisoned, and I'm ashamed to be seen like this. Was I ever someone who walked outside and went about his business, received someone else's gaze intentionally into his own eyes and spoke and was made to do work and...it doesn't make sense, it's all just mockery and humiliation. There's nothing visibly wrong with me. There's no reason, so there's no way to know if the pain and helplessness will all disappear in a few hours or go on forever. If I can get far enough inside my memories, I can get away, any direction as long as it's away from here. I know the inside of the black hole isn't filled with golden light, with August days, with the loving faces of people I pushed away long before they died. I helplessly watched myself push...

I can't. That's not helping me.

So does the particle in my brain feel any of this, or communicate it instantly to the others it's entangled with, and receive any of the muted warmth and glimmer of the earth's sun that filters in here to me, the air surrounding me set trembling by dead voices? Does it get that in the void, anywhere? There's no reason it should, should it? Any more than there is reason for me to believe with every fiber of my being that I'm the ghost haunting black hole NGC 1313 X-2 right now. But then again there's no reason for this convulsive pain in my foot, is there, and yet all the same HERE IT FUCKING IS.

Her face in the doorway and fading as she retires back into the hall, her dim blue mummu like a shroud. That's the only face I've seen here, so she must be the one who helps me.

She's probably the one who helps me, but I've seen another face here besides hers. It was in a sort of square, I think, like a frame, maybe my own face in a mirror? A bathroom mirror? Streaked with steam? I'm not sure, it did resemble my face, but it was also like hers. When do I steam up the mirror here? Or was it not here?

The face was full of pain, so it had to have been mine. But, it seems to me in hindsight that there was too much pain in that face for it to be mine. In my memory, I see not so much a face in pain, as pain taking on a face.

At Dr. Shitansky's request, we've all gathered in the middle of the auditorium. Everyone but Dr. Corngholm, anyway. And her father. Maybe he wandered off on her again. Or did I just dream that I met him? Allegre and Dr. Liu have assembled a series of cumbersome devices on a pair of tables from the old cafeteria, and they're about to demonstrate them. First, though, by Dr. Shitansky's orders, we all have to pull papery white clean room coveralls on over our clothes. Once zipped up, I'm completely covered, except for my face. There's nothing for Bas to wear, so he's been sealed into an expensive-looking ventilated carrier, and all you can see of him is his staring face in a tiny window.

"I got everybody these cool sunglasses," Allegre says, producing a cardboard carton. Everyone but Renbrui, who's wearing her calming goggles, puts them on. They're white with golden-brown lenses.

"OK, so this array is a cubic interferometric ablative laser spectroscopy device," he says, spreading his hands to indicate all the equipment, which looks a lot like an old tube amplifier and stereo hi fi gear strung together with thick cables.

Was I dreaming, or did I really get up and walk down the hall to the window, and see the blue-black sky all white with stars? I remember the coolness of the walls and the floor against my hands and the soles of my bare feet.

"Dr. Liu and I designed it to locate the entangled particle," he goes on. "It does this by generating an interferometric field in the form of a cubical laser that should encompass all of TISH."

He takes on a sort of hectoringly reassuring tone.

"Now this field is completely harmless to us, but, just in case, we've asked you to wear this protective gear for the duration of the test. There should be no residual effects, no radiation or anything like that. If, however, in the next few days or so, you do feel any unusual physical uh, physical symptoms, then you should get yourself checked, just to be sure."

He sits down on a folding chair, and Dr. Liu stands up.

"So first of all I would like to thank Engineer Allegre for his incredible help with the interferometer. This is an especially difficult mechanism to make when you do not have access to computers. Yes, this is a completely analogue interferometer, it's 'old-school,' ha ha. What it will do when we turn it on is produce a laser field that none of us (hopefully, ha ha) will be able to feel or to see, although there is a slight chance you could experience maybe a little tingling. The field will sweep from the lowest to the highest frequency the device can generate. If the particle is affected by a certain frequency, we should detect the interference, and we can roughly localize it to probably about thirty meters of the machine."

Allegre adds, from his seat,

"Basically, we're looking for the frequency of the particle. If the field soaks it up, then we can find where it is."

Dr. Shitansky turns to us and says—"Given its entanglement with a particle in a black hole, the particle here may well absorb energy at the frequency available to it. So, we're looking for a hole in the data."

"Technically," Dr. Liu says, "since there is a certain amount of void in any object, and actually most of any object is empty space, we are looking for a surplus of nothing, ha ha."

"Anything that's more nothing than usual for objects," Allegre says from his seat.

After calling for questions, and getting none, Dr. Liu continues.

"Let's get going. Again, if you're feeling anything out of the ordinary, please let us know."

Visible waves of heat are already rising from the equipment, which emits a strong smell of roasting insulation. Dr. Liu takes her position alongside Dr. Shitansky at the readout station, which is a series of paper tape tickers, while Allegre will be moving all around and among the machinery to prevent explosions. He crouches down by a sizeable steel console shaped like a giant horseshoe crab, and locks eyes with Dr. Shitansky.

"Begin experiment," Dr. Shitansky says.

At this signal, Allegre throws stiff switches and turns big knobs. A deep, ragged whir, abrupt and very loud, rises from the machines.

"Enlapsement underway," Dr. Liu says.

There's a rumble like thunder indoors, like the sound of an approaching storm coming from inside the house, moving from room to room and along the hall. The device shifts from one frequency to another with heavy clunks, followed by modifications of the whirring note, which opens out into a deepening chord, a sweeping tongue of sound that moves back and forth inside the expanding harmony. For a moment, as the frequency rolls through one of these changes, something goes right through me—like the dreamy, rootless feeling you get when you're standing waist deep in the ocean and a swell rolls around you. My body rises up on my toes and my eyes roll back into my head. It's like I've turned into one of those toy dolls that stick out their tongues and bug out their eyes when you squeeze them. Then the feeling passes and I sink back down into my former posture. The ocean swell force sloshes, staying close to me. When it wobbles nearer, my eyes roll up a little, my body lifts onto its toes slightly, and when it teeters away again, I settle back as I was.

I'm breathing heavily; not rapidly, but with effort. No one seems to notice, to be aware of me—all eyes are on the tapes streaming from the recorder. I hear an unfamiliar voice say—

"it's spiritual...he's like..."

The voice wafts up and passes me, as if the speaker were drifting by on a platform. A black woman's voice.

"—at the reception...asked me to..."

That voice, also a woman's, older, and acoustically flattened, as if she were speaking right up against a wall. The voice is continuous for a few seconds, but only those words are intelligible.

Again the wave—much stronger—terrifyingly strong—swinging me up to the top of the drop on a roller coaster that's just the earth, nothing I can escape, because the height and the drop are inside me.

Dr. Liu says "There's some geometric compression and desync—"

I see white ribbony flames around needles of pale gloom sliding sideways across my field of vision, more like an insistent memory than a hallucination.

"—that should be preliminary to lapse."

The flames extend and contract as I sway on my feet, like light reflecting off a crinkled, glossy surface.

"No gaps yet...but some widening here..."

Here it comes now—the lightless, clairvoyant weight at the bottom of NGC 1313's midnight.

"Lapse, right there!"

The timbre of the thunder takes on a brassy quality that makes it sound imploring. My vision flickers in and out, but my hearing is sharpening itself, taking in steadily lower and lower frequencies. I'm trying to listen, but every time my vision flashes I feel the drag of my body, and when it goes dark, that goes numb. Each pulse brings vision and weight back, on my way to the floor. The sound is constant. It isn't a voice and it doesn't speak, but it means things.

The sky darkened around us; his appearance didn't change, but he's suddenly unrecognizable—I can't find him, my sense impression and the voice I hear is like every voice and none and there and speaking words like any words but they might as well be musical notes and a new instrument like a song from between planets that no amount of ingenuity could invent. My own   shot   from out of h aven errify aid of me, it doesn't   go back to being me   the last   ven is bea   irre allu   out of the   music   not me irra   ith ompas   never 'd ayting ny t b   ie on my side   lying and lying on my side   legs lying   arms fold

"There's signal failure on two!" Allegre says.

"Strong lapse obtusion at 7:55," Dr. Liu says.

I'm looking across to Renbrui. Everyone else is bent over the recorders. She's the only one who's noticed there's something wrong with me. She indifferently turns her head away, back to watching the others, but I don't know if she turns her eyes away, or her mind. Like the curl of a waterfall seen from above, a distinct line traces the wavering contour of Renbrui's face as she turns it away, until the cascade of her hair veils it, and leaves me remembering.

"Just a minute, just a minute," she says. "Your A23 forms go in this basket. Your B17 forms go in this basket. Which one of you is Gross?"

The music is playing.

"You had better have all your shit."

I recognize her light and shade—the light and shade of old trees, old summer, old sunlight, the ancient fragrances of young wildflowers, the embarrassing honey of youth parcelled up and chambered in combs of past time. A space opens when she turns her head, my memories unlace and mingle with hers like shining beads strung on one string, coiling down into the hole to be destroyed. Each bead has the light and color of a different night or day. There's a bare razor blade clipped against the pages in the clipboard.

I see the rim of a crater in the road, I see her forearm, I see her hand holding a pistol, I smell powder, I smell car exhaust, a submerged frenzy, wind whips long strands of hair across the face, I hear Dr. Shitansky's voice ask an indistinct question, I see myself on the road—

"There's a geometric dilation of the failure on two," Dr. Shitansky says.

"There may be some lapse flow from two to five," Dr. Liu says.

I see blood on the razor blade. The pain in my foot explodes, it's like it's burst apart and the bones have split open—her thin lips and delicate teeth white and red around the pure darkness of her mouth, pain, gnawing my foot like acid eating into metal, oh my heart—there she goes, across pale mirror sands of a dead level flat desert, hair billowing from her head like incense, and my head pulped in a stone basin by a downpour of transparent lead Renbrui faces. What am I crossing? Heaving string waves whose ends are caught on the god-reel of a black brane, reeling them in. Bas is staring at me. Does he see what I see? He has his left eye turned toward the little window in his carrier and he's got it fixed on me, a lustrous, living pupil there.

From somewhere else in the building comes the sound of fluttering wings, like a bird, a large one, has gotten inside, trapped maybe. The flap of its wings rebounds off the walls of one of the apartments, maybe in the stairwell. I want to get up. I want to go look. If it needs help to escape, I want to help it. Or if it's hurt. There's a harried, frantic note in the sound. The bird is afraid. It might be a hawk, or a vulture, dangerous. Turn over, on my stomach, then swing my legs off the bed, out into the air. This air is steamy, filled with steam. I push myself upright on my normal foot and snatch, fumble, grab at my crutches, cram them back into my chafed armpits. Lope forward now, bad foot crooked up, heave toward the door, out into the hall. Follow the wing noise. Pass the bathroom. The door is open. Don't look inside. Don't look for the tub, the figure, the razor blade in blood on the floor.

My story has finished with me, and it's going to leave me now. I had, at Dr. Shitansky's insistence, installed a land line at home, and plugged in the old black rotary telephone she'd given me. The peal of its ringer nearly threw me out of my chair. Dr. Shitansky's flat, level voice on the other end, a report I had to do by Monday, type up, report, type, have to pick it up, go back to TISH...

"I don't have a key..."

"Renbrui will open the door for you."

The place was dark when I pulled in. The time was about seven PM. Darkness, silence. But the front door was open. It jangled and clattered as I pulled it toward me—a keychain, a wad of dozens of keys, dangled from the lock. Renbrui's keychain.

I let the door wheeze to behind me. I withdrew the key and set the chain down out of sight, below the counter of the reception desk where I had once turned in my application to work here.

Renbrui is in the darkened corridor, sitting on the floor.

"Are you OK?"

She lifts her head without turning to look at me.

"I'm fine, Gross. I am ship-shape."

I squat down by her.

"Do you sit here on the floor, in the dark, often?"

"No, Gross. I have never done this before."

The wind rises and lowers again, rattling the leaves beyond the windows.

"Why are you doing it now?"

She keeps her eyes on her feet, sticking straight out ahead of her, with her skirt spread evenly over her legs. She takes a deep breath.

"Well Gross, you see, there's a first time for everything."

I notice her goggles lying on the ground by her right hand.

I feel a spasm in my foot—the old wound. I shift myself, sit down directly on the floor, take my foot in my hand and squeeze it.

"I'm sorry about that, Gross."

She sounds it.

"It was an accident. It's OK."

I can feel the earth settle. Its gravity.

"What's wrong?"

She waits a long time.

"I have cancer in my brain, Gross."

Through the window, the leaves teeter and then fall still again.

"I've been to six specialists. They all say I'm fine, just fine. But I know. I'm not fine. It's cancer."

"Do you mean they say you have cancer, but it's not serious?"

"No, Gross," she says with some of her old disdain. "I mean I *have* cancer and they say I *don't*. *That's* what I mean. The hole gave it to me. It gave me brain cancer."

She clasps her hands together, squeezing them so tightly I can hear them creak.

"Or hadn't you noticed?"

"I've noticed you've been troubled…"

She rubs her face, her forehead.

"I'm always dizzy."

I force myself to look away. I knead my left foot.

"It's going to kill me."

I'm thinking that some dark radiation was pouring out from beneath her hood of hair, as it fell forward about her face, endless, bottomless, irreparable misery, when she abruptly looks up at me, drives her face directly towards mine, catches my lips in hers—cold, dry, the sudden fragrance of her hair all around me—her face pulls away again—the mouth says—

"Shut up—just shut up."

She reaches into the purse lying beside her. A flash of nickel plating in the gloom as she puts the barrel up against her temple —a bang and a flash. She slumps toward me. Topples over onto her side. Her head clunks against the floor. A black halo seeps from her hair. It spreads, and gleams. In a moment, that dark, liquid edge will reach me.

Later, her open mouth will remind me of a crisp-edged hole burned in a piece of paper. But, by then, there won't be anything but anguish left of me, to see it.

Out there, coming down the canyon, following the narrow dirt path, the white thread, gliding along upright, exactly my height, homing in on me. It glides along the ground and sometimes it's jerky, like a hair dancing along the bottom of the movie, and then when I look again it's less definite, more like a twirling, narrow column of white smoke. The smell of powder smoke, the crater in the highway, I see Renbrui beside it, a pistol glinting in her hand, the bright sunshine concentrated into a thin gleam running down the barrel to the black hole at the end, and what I'm seeing is a string, a particle, with all its bonus dimensions that I shouldn't be able to perceive, a string that must end on the black brane, NGC1313 X-2. Death—or maybe not death but death's herald—strictly and smoothly following the kinked dirt path toward me, and I don't know why running should help, but I have to run from it, even with a shitfoot I have to run. Staggered on my crutches, the call of a bird echoes in the empty rooms around me, the reflected light of the thread gathers around me—I don't dare look back, the thread is coming. I've got to go.

The road or path fans out in front of me to the horizon, widens to fill the world. The light spills along the daybreak like a kind of leaking, a sky-leak, and in the watery light that precedes the fire and pink and golden orange, I'm staggering away on a foot that feels like it's cycling through different broken bones, trying to get by with one crutch and sort of swimming in sick air, clammy and stifling, keep going, cold sweat, nausea, pain-nausea and referred pain. If I move fast, it's because I'm afraid. Cold sweat makes me fast. Fast and sloppy. Staring at the horizon, as if staring would make a place for me

there. Whatever I'm staring at is where I'm going anyway, and there'll be a hidden bolus of fury and anguish cached for me there, like supplies, if I can keep stepping through the genres to reach it. As the sun comes up I've got purple and fuschia veils dangling around my face like objective lens flares. I've been inside for so long the sunlight is destroying my vision. Everything is gold and suffused with ominous brown light that fades into itself as it limbers up.

I gaze dispassionately through the tinted window of my hotel room as the city lights come on, nursing a drink, my foot propped on a chair. I raise the glass to my lips with a shaking hand and it bangs against my teeth. A gleam beneath the folds of my discarded newspaper on the table next to me. I draw the paper away with my free hand. There's a silver pistol lying there, its barrel toward me. Time to go.

I take a cab to the airport, hobble through security to my gate. I'm allowed to pre-board. They're fetching my wheelchair when one of the gate staff approaches me with a concerned expression.

"I'm sorry, but at this time we *will* have to deny you passage. I'm afraid I can't give you any further information, but your ticket price *has* been refunded, ok?"

She hands me a print-out that instructs me to go directly to the border service office in the main terminal. That's where they'll arrest me.

Somehow I get myself back to passenger drop-off and a cab stand. Beside the kiosk, there's a heavyset woman indifferently directing passengers to cabs, giving each one a folded sheet of paper as they pass her. The phone in the kiosk rings. Reaching through the window, she answers it without leaving her place. She listens, nods, looks down the line, sees me, and says something into the phone. I wait for her to hang up—I can't just go, not without a plan, somewhere to go to. There are only three people ahead of me now, more cabs coming. I pretend to fumble in my bags, to play for time, trying to look bored, my eyes going everywhere.

There's a city bus loading passengers, the last one is just boarding now. I lunge forward, hauling my bag, stopping a car as I hobble over to the bus, waving. I climb up and in and we pull out into traffic. I see the woman at the cab stand hurrying into the kiosk. Will she know the number of the bus?

I get off at the first stop outside the airport, find myself in a terrifying, abandoned industrial area with windblown trash and cars on blocks. I find another stop on a different line and wait two hours for another bus, my foot throbbing on top of my bag.

It's a long ride. Finally we pass a twenty-four hour coffee shop and I get off at the nearest stop and stagger back to it. They still have pay phones here; the coffee shop even has proper booths in the back. I get through. It'll cost me, but I can get a driver to take me as far as the coast. It's been years and years, and days and days, and the unremitting pain in my foot is not like an old friend now, it's every bit the fucking bitch it's always been, but at least no worse. The face in the bathroom mirror is the same, too, in the scratched and pitted glass: strained, unshaven, hollow-eyed, frightened, hopeless, old.

I'm back in my booth, waiting on the pickup, when three guys come tumbling in, laughing and swatting each other on the back. They were cleaners at TISH. I almost didn't recognize them out of their custodial utility outfits. Now they're all dressed like racing touts, in stingy-brim hats, bright plaid blazers, gaudy neckties with gold tie bars and flashy cufflinks. They see me almost immediately and come piling into my booth with loud and hearty greetings like I'm an old pal, shaking me by the shoulder, grinning gold teeth, a smell of cigarettes, pomade and aftershave. They seem genuinely pleased to see me.

"Hand me a buck and a quarter..."

"In a pig's ear!"

They go over my paperwork.

"The old style!"

They approve of the way I've filled out the forms.

"Hey come have a look at these!"

"Now that's more like it! Swell!"

"That's the way it's done!"

I tell them I'm waiting for a car.

"A car?!"

One of them goes to the back, and enters the phone booth.

"Listen mac, you don't want to go on any drive right now."

"I—I have to go, to get out..."

"*We'll* get you out, chum! You just leave it to us, huh? Now, what do say—who looks good for tomorrow?"

He pulls a racing form from his breast pocket, cracking his chewing gum.

"Water Blanding to win in the first. *That* is a *cinch*."

"OK."

I gaze dispassionately through the tinted window of my hotel room, down at streets of gold in the Book of Life District, then up toward the black peak of the Mountain of Sleep. They got me out, those guys, after all. Good fellows. I toss back the rest of my whiskey. Venetian blinds stripe my face. My foot feels like it's been run over. Pain hasn't made me cool. The stripes on my face lay bars across streams of cold sweat. The whiskey I drink knots itself into a neat acrid little bundle inside me. It sure doesn't help.

The Book of Life district is scintillating with thousands of delicate little lanterns. The streets of El Dorado are beaded with light, and stately couples promenade from bead to bead, an unofficial nightly ritual, the post-prandial stroll, a time for small talk, check in, how is your family, what's the weather like in the south right now, have you eaten? There are no cars in the city. Instead, there are purely decorative phantom highways consisting of transparent pipes suspended in the air, filled with flowing water. Glowing bulbs of all different colors circulate around the city in these pipes, so the whole place seems alive with seething traffic. I know the gleaming line is whirling toward me through the dark, up and down the streets like these promenaders, in no hurry, tireless, coming for me.

I've contacted NGC 1 3 1 3. Tomorrow I head for the mountains, where the Refuge of the Trunkless Torso guards a pass known as the Trunkless Gate, the only way out of the country's interior. Daladara has arranged for me to pick up the packet I'll need to get through, a sort of omamori-bag with a talisman knotted up neatly inside it, and you can't ever open the bag or see what's inside.

Down in the streets, there's a white thread hunting for me. If I flip open this copy LIFE magazine here, and drop my finger on a phrase at random, I'll know what it's thinking.

"I came with my ministers," the magazine says.

I know that at least one of them is working here at the hotel, trying to locate me, which is why I haven't budged from my room—and I won't, not until it's time to break out. The table beside me is still bare, I've torn the pillows from my bed so no gleaming steel barrel can coagulate under any of them. I've set the little trash can out in the hall and filled the ice bucket with tap water. I flip over the newspaper—nothing beneath it. The headline reads THREE MORE COUNTRY

VILLAS BURN, WILD MEN CLAIM RESPON-
SIBILITY.

My head keeps going up levels, I can't stop it. I want to keep both feet planted flat on the floor, but it's no good—my left foot...Prop it up on the windowsill for a while. Watch my reflection become distinct in the darkening glass, a godlike ghost materializing over the city. Yes, you're the god of your life—does it matter? I'm going to see that thread in the streets dart behind my face, feel it tickle as it pinches off my heart and rips open the blood vessels in my brain with one savage wrench that will destroy my memories, my language, my senses, my consciousness. I think about standing up to draw the curtains and it makes me breathe heavily, and my head droops, but then I rally somehow, get up and do it. You won't get me that way. Not by reflection magic in windows.

Now I have a golden curtain to stare at, with its shadowy troughs and glittering folds. I can count each identical one. How many waves? How many times will you come back to me before you stop coming back to me? Somewhere in the future, there's a number. This many times, and no more. It's an unknown number, and it's a definite number. It is certain and uncertain. I reach for my tumbler, but it's not there. Was I drinking? Maybe that was a different night, in some other hotel. I get to not have a clear sense of time, because I'm on the run. Very slowly and painfully on the run.

A noise behind me. I turn, and see an envelope lying on the floor just inside the room. It's clear that someone has just thrust it beneath the door. A manila envelope with a huge cream-colored postage stamp on it, and plainly not a bill or message from the hotel. It lies there as if it had always been there, like I'm looking at a carefully-arranged photograph, designed to be a kind of riddle. With a sigh, I lever myself onto my feet and make my way over. I pick up the envelope and throw myself down onto the bed.

The stamp has borders of paper lace. It's emblazoned with the symbol of the city, a man on horseback entering a gate, in squashed perspective. The image is so stylized that I have trouble making it out. It's almost a pictogram, and at first all I can see is a childish doodle, a drawing of a scarcely discernible face with clown-like tufts of hair, pinched, squinting eyes, a drawling, full-lipped mouth.

The document inside is printed on heavy paper, almost cardboard, and all in Ehepaar. The language has been written in its own alphabet since some kind of quasi-revolution back in the sixties; airy blocks of characters, crooks, dots, horizontal lines, and lots of what look like little capital T's under other characters. I can't tell if it reads side to side or up and down, what's punctuation and what's a letter. The overall impression is that I'm looking at fish hooks and springs fitted together like mosaic tiles to form rectangular zones. There's a typed note in English, too. I suspect it is a translation of the other document.

The note refers to the coordinated authority extension service of a quorum of the local myriarchies. From what I can gather, the city has several governancies, depending on what neighborhood you're in, and their duties partially overlap in ways that are subject to frequent renegotiation. Many of the officials are solely occupied with these redistributions of responsibilities and perennial readjustments. Apparently, I've now missed too many meetings. What meetings? There's little I can glean from the translation, if that's what it is; the language is decorous and off-balance, with oddly inharmonious word choices. They say that my "dereliction" could be "miscontrived as insouciance," for example. It's like a coherent sentence ran afoul of a thesaurus. From what I can make out, this is an unofficial summons to a casual discussion about my propensity to miss meetings of "vital import." So that sucks. I know I don't want to go do that.

I set the envelope and its contents on the nightstand and roll onto my side, one leg lying on top of the other, one arm under the pillow, and, for the first time in I don't know how long, I'm relaxed. It's like a blessing. I sleep. Outside, the day breaks, the sun rises, the road that vanishes into the mountains becomes visible again out of the night. Everyone I know is there, heading out, throwing off a long, settling cloud of dust. Heading out, away from me. I want to run after them and call to them, but the voice of the black brane holds me back. Even though it never talks, I have to listen for it, in case it does. I'm being held back by a voice I've never heard, saying words it hasn't said. I don't call out. I don't raise a finger, even as my soul begs them not to abandon me, and the faces of the people I loved, and who have died, resonate in the ruins of my brain like a song that I'll never stop singing to myself, now that there's no one to sing it to me. I don't ever want to stop missing them or mourning them. And meantime everyone alive I let go. How can I ask you to stay, when I can't even point to one thing worth staying for? Just point to the nothing where there's supposed to be me. A nothing that loves you.

I don't want to dream this, I don't want to dream at all, or no, I want only to dream. Or if I wake up, let me wake up all at once, right now, right into the dream of whatever my day is, whatever *this* is, just don't let me hang in the between where I can actually see what's there. Let me be awake or asleep but not waking—I'll go insane. More insane.

When I do wake up, the light is the same. I think the clock is the same. It feels as though I've slept a long time, but it also seems as though I've only just been out for a few minutes. Someone is sitting in the chair by the window, and for an instant I think it's me, but it's not anything like me. It's a small person of uncertain gender, all in black, neat as a pin, neatly folded hands on neatly folded legs. Dark hair, crisply parted and sleeked down, a broad brow and a wry expression. Orson Welles, Dorothy Parker, age eleven.

"Ehrscoep," the person says, in a hoarse, tenor voice. That's the neutral greeting in Ehepaar. Everything about this person is neutral, and that reassures me.

"Do you know who I am?" they ask, in lightly accented English.

I remember Daladara's instructions.

"Are you in Dub Tables?"

"Yes."

"Have you ever been to Misirbris?"

"Never."

"What do you have?"

"Gorgons. My name is Fragrant Thread."

Fragrant Thread answered all the questions correctly and with the bemusement of an adult humoring a precocious child.

"I'm Gross," I say.

"I've brought you this data," Fragrant Thread says, and lightly thumps a little box on the table beside them. It looks like a velveted ring box.

"And I've been enjoined to answer your questions about it and its use. My first responsibility, which I discharge now, it to remind you that to open this box even slightly is to put an end to its usefulness immediately and for all time. Further, it is incumbent upon me to advise you that to open this box even slightly will entail additional risk to you, the nature of which cannot be predicted. This is in addition to the loss of utility I have already mentioned. Please, let me know now if you have fully understood what I have just told you."

Fragrant Thread enunciated these words carefully, with distinct pauses. When they asked if I understood, they spoke with earnest solicitude.

"I understand."

Fragrant Thread sits there, evidently waiting for me to go on.

"Don't open the box."

Fragrant Thread continues waiting. I can hear a bell ringing the hour down in the District of the Book of Life.

"Opening the box, even a little, will make it useless, and lead to more problems."

Fragrant Thread nods.

"If you have further questions, I am at your disposal for a little while. Though, when the quarter strikes next, we must be away."

"So soon?"

"Yes."

I struggle to get up.

"Do I have time to get my things?"

"You will not be detained. You will be able to return here after we're done."

A note of derision in their voice, as though I were a disappointment.

Fragrant Thread leads me outside. They're so small, it's strange that they're not more easily lost in the crowd. The streets here are always thronged with people going about their business, delivering everything in the world; there are hordes of gawking tourists and daily processions by the Valentinians or the devotees of Werunos and Harben, or World War Three or the Sakyamunists or Santeria or the Fifth Monarchists or something new, or just processions for their own sakes sometimes. I think the citizens here have processing in their blood. They just do it, and the pretexts supply themselves.

Fragrant Thread leads me around to the far side of the hotel. City life in El Dorado revolves around an artificial hill. Its official name is (checks guidebook) Civic-Cultural Bioplant District Center One, but everyone calls it Technomound. The hill is surrounded at its base by a nest of restaurants, dance clubs, and concert venues. There are two funicular lines, one on the north side and the other on the west side where we are, leading up to the top. Once you get there, you can rent some kind of pedal vehicle for pocket change and ride it down again, going round and round or using switchbacks, as you see fit. At dusk, the bicycles and tricycles are all faintly luminous, so that, from a distance, the hill looks like a cascade of ghosts is whirling down its slopes. If you would rather walk, there are of course walkways too. The hill is landscaped in terraced sculpture gardens, and there's a light show every week at the summit. It's always thronged with people, and that's where Fragrant Thread leads me. I've never been there.

We get our ticket and squeeze aboard the west slope funicular car. I've wedged myself against the door frame so I can lean, taking weight off my bad foot. My crutch is useful when it comes to making room. Through the windows I can see huge trees and flower beds sweep by beneath us, the neat spiral path with its cyclists, the walkways of dawdling pedestrians, and the city beyond, dim indigo shapes in a thin haze under a rich blue sky.

The funicular stops, the doors open, and we spring out. I have to shuffle out and to the side, avoiding the press of passengers. The peak is broad, spacious, and most of the passengers head directly to the bicycle rental racks, so not many visitors actually stay or spend much time up here. Fragrant Thread smiles at me wanly, and waves me on. We're heading for one of the lookout bays, where people can gaze out like gods over the city.

The intuition grows steadily on me, like a low, fluting murmur coming and going down a long, empty street. And now uneasiness begins to drone on top of that. This is a cul de sac. The only way out of here is back down, using a slow funicular or an even slower bicycle with one foot out of commission. I have stepped blindly into a trap.

I remember what Daladara told me to do. I can't hold back without tipping my hand. That wouldn't do. Here's the scenic vista. There are a few tables and chairs set out, some coin-operated binoculars. When Fragrant Thread is not looking my way, I grab my pen and notebook, flip to a blank page, pull the cap, ready to go.

Fragrant Thread waves me over to a remote bench, overlooking a dazzling expanse of tall trees scintillating in the mountain wind and Fragrant Thread's black form embossed on the scene.

"Just a second!" I say, throwing myself into a seat.

I immediately begin drawing a kaikalak—that's a diamond with two horns sprouting from each corner, long horns to the right and left, short at top and bottom, all without lifting the nib or my eyes from the page, the way Daladara told me to do it.

"If your intuition is trying to tell you something, draw a kaikalak. If someone is giving you a bad feeling, do it in their presence, while they're still close. Do it like this...keep the pen on the paper. This is Zaman Wislin. Nothing will happen if nothing's wrong, but if something is wrong, you can get out of it by doing this."

I finish drawing and raise my eyes.

The daylight dims around Fragrant Thread. The wind stops. The leaves on the trees are motionless. The world is silent. Fragrant Thread's face is expressionless, composed, and dead-eyed.

"You shouldn't have done that," he says. Fragrant Thread's voice is suddenly masculine.

I burst out in a cold sweat, fear grabs my stomach. This whole thing isn't real. That's the problem. It's also the solution, though. I jerk up out of my seat and the pain in my left foot shrills at me.

"You can't move!" I say. "You can't!"

I'm trying to believe it. I brandish the notebook, flapping the open page at Fragrant Thread.

"I trusted you!"

His outline becomes unnaturally precise, his features become harder and harder, even as the color drains from them. He stares at me with a corpse's eyes. I hear him speak, but his face doesn't move. The more distinct he is, the more false he is. The voice is circling me, speaking unintelligible words in the rasped and warping pitches of a detuned shortwave radio.

"You can't break the dream!" I say, warning them, trying to make sure it's true, feeling completely ridiculous.

"You can't break it!"

I'm backing away. The longer I can stand it, the harder it will be for him to follow me. The pain in my foot keeps gouging holes in the spell; I lean on it. Biting my lips, grimacing, I back out of there, finally turn and make a break for the rental bikes. I throw the jewelry box in the garbage. My spine goes cold and I get the idea that something has been waiting for me up there in the sky above the mound, and it's reaching down, it wants to snatch me up into the sky.

I shove a bunch of weird local coins into the coin box and dislodge one of the tricycles. Pumping with one foot, standing, using my weight, the crutch thrown across my handlebars, I merge in with the others and start rolling back down the slope. I use the switchbacks to get down more rapidly. Bright patches alternate with shadowy passages, colorful flower beds, sombre lanes of cypresses like huge black candles, surrounded by people—relaxed people, who laugh and make small talk, dilly dally along, taking in the sights, pause to shade their eyes and look out over the city as I frantically descend past them, not daring to look behind me, knowing that sky-thing gropes after me, probes in among the branches to try to find me. I have to resist the temptation to push ahead as fast as I can go—which is not so fast—because I need these people around me. I don't think anything bad can happen if there are witnesses. Stay with them, but leap frog from group to group, as one bunch slows or stops to admire a statue or take a picture, drive on to the next. Just don't stop. Get down off this thing.

As I reach the base, all my energy dissipates. I return the tricycle, locking it into its frame, and lead against it. Am I about to pass out? I can't do that. Walking with a crutch is wearing me out. I have to go. Out, through the turnstile, to the street. Get a cab. That's what you do. Make them say follow that car. But—no cars here. You take a cycle-rickshaw thing instead.

An idea I had previously rejected as kind of dumb recurs to me. I stop and lean against a palm tree, pull out my pocket street map of the city and check the index. I find 1313 North Grand Concourse. It's a real address. So, I flag down a cycle-rickshaw, climb painfully into the back, and give the number to my cyclist. As we pull away, I'm swiveling my stiff neck—no sign of Fragrant Thread. The sky seems very close, something in it, invisible, searches.

After about half an hour of weaving we arrive at an apartment building. I pay my cyclist and confront three enormously wide, deep storyes of unrepentant brown concrete. I buzz apartment X-2 and the door bolt snaps back after a brief delay. The noise is so loud I can't be sure if there was a voice on the intercom as well.

The vestibule is empty and very still. I hear only the whirring of the air ducts. White lettering on artificial wood signs mounted on the walls indicate which apartments are in which directions. The windowless halls are very wide, with alternating stretches of even fluorescent lighting and shadowy zones. Thin carpet everywhere, brown with broad orange and yellow ribbons, edged in pale red. This building could be anywhere. There's no sense of the city outside at all. Tepid, dry air, museum smell. Dark brown apartment doors with white numbers on fake wood medallions.

I knock at X-2. The walk took me so long I wonder if they've forgotten me, but the door opens. There's a little foyer in there, all painted a pale yellow, with a big brown wooden flower clock hanging on the wall, and a little table with an orange pitcher of artificial flowers in it. An old man stands there in evening clothes. His face is lean, with sunken, clean-shaven cheeks. His full lips and the area around his lips, as well as part of the tip of his nose, are frostbitten and discolored. Between his jutting brow and high cheekbones, his deep-set eyes are completely obscured.

"Are you Fragrant Thread?" I ask.

Only his hand and arm move, whisking a frostbitten index finger to his lips. I expect him to invite me into his apartment, but he steps out into the hallway with me and carefully shuts the door to X-2 behind him. He then gestures down the hall, not the way I came, but further on, and we begin to walk together. He towers over me, slightly clumsy, as if his joints were all loose. We walk, and go on walking. This is a problem, since I was counting on the use of his bathroom.

We walk for a long time, in silence. The corridor stretches on and on, in and out of brief dark patches, turning corners at regular intervals. I try to imagine what it's like to live in this morguelike, ominous building. You tiptoe from room to room, not daring to make any noise. Who's listening? Who's watching? Everyone, nobody. Anyone. You, for example. You listen, you watch. You jump at the chance to catch a glimpse of a neighbor. You live quietly, very quietly. Carefully, like a monk or a nun. Like a monk or a nun living in a place they only suspect might have other monks and nuns living in it.

"Is there a bathroom I can use?" I blurt, finally.

The old man pauses. It's only as he turns, smiling, to face me that I become aware of his sadness and weariness. He gazes into my eyes, swings his arm up and lightly taps my skull just behind my right ear. Tap tap tap. His arm drops back down to his side and we resume walking. Five minutes later, apparently concluding that I need further prompting, he stops again, holds his open palm up in front of my face, then produces from behind my right ear a shimmering black coin about the size of a quarter that he shows me and then tucks into my shirt pocket. Again, he resumes walking. The coin is cold against my chest. I think he's telling me to listen to the black hole. I've been in contact, I am in contact. Very gradually, the pressure begins to ease.

We're still walking. The monotony and silence of the hallway lulls me into a daydream. I'm thinking now about the time I first saw Renbrui after her attack. The weekend came between. I saw her from my desk. She was outside, pacing up and down, eating a little triangular sandwich. As she moved back and forth, the shining fronds of the plants that surround the building stirred and flickered like muddy green flames between us. There was something unbelievable about the way she looked. It was impossible to get used to her, at least for me. I didn't think anyone else at TISH noticed her much, but I did. There was no way not to. She's perfect, and even now, with her goggles, wherever she is, she's still uncannily, subtly perfect. If only she hadn't been. I can see her, walking along calmly, her problems—whatever they were—are at bay.

If life stops me going one way, all I can do is go another way.

Shining city of annulment, of white lintels, a blue sky like an island in time; that is, it sets the time, undetermined by any other thing or power apart from blue sky. Its beauty is already painful, even without the anguish of knowing I can't experience it, not for real. Even if I could see its beauty with my own eyes, that wouldn't mean being it, both it and me at once.

This is just idle talk. It's not ineffable or inexplicable, it's just incoherent. I'm still waiting on the black brane to string it together on the other side of the event horizon. Then it will make sense, make all too much sense. So what's left? Sad people with their sad choices seen sadly.

Suddenly, the old man's palm presses lightly against the center of my back. He veers off toward the right side of the hallway, steering me like a dance partner. There's a very faint noise that I now realize I've been hearing for a long time. He hasn't actually been silent at all; he's been murmuring, speaking continuously in the soft voice of air in ventilator ducts.

"...the having discarded it is the talisman," I think I hear him say as he puts me through a door no different from any of the others we've been passing. I emerge into a stone room with fresh air tossing in and out of tall sunny windows. This isn't the same building.

The old man is shutting the door between us as I turn back to look, and I see him make a plunging gesture with his right hand, pointing me on. Then the door is closed in deep black shadow. The room is bare, not large, and there's a few steps leading up to a portal that admits in a clear shaft of light. I can't find the door I came through. I don't think it's there anymore.

Out through that portal, the only way to go. It leads me up to a terrace overlooking the plateau. El Dorado glitters like a heap of diamonds, miles and miles away.

The building I've just emerged from is a sprawling edifice of massive stone blocks, festooned with colorful pennants; it all has a strangely lightweight look, though, and the sunlight striking it is like moonbeams.

I'm in the mountains. I'm at the Refuge. I feel a pang of

regret as I look back toward the city, but the street hustle I'm nostalgic for was something I only ever imagined.

Then I see the white line flicker on the road below, one end on the ground, and the other darting frenetically in the air as it comes. A spasm of dread hits me. The walls of the Refuge float beneath my hands—it's like there's broken glass grating between the bones of my feet and I yelp and whimper as I walk.

I drop the frostbitten black quarter into a coin slot in the wall and the door, little more than a metal flap, unlatches with a far-away click. I push through metal flaps on stiff hinges. I hurry, blindly. Now and then I catch a glimpse of one of the mathetes who live here doing their translations in the dark.

I emerge into the blinding sun again. A staggering view of the pass below. The funicular car that runs down into the mountain shadows stands open for me and I throw myself in. The door closes, and the empty car lurches from its dock and rolls down the cable, swaying and creaking.

At the bottom, I'll take some kind of car or tram to the flatter, open country. The mountains might slow the thread for a while. Cold sweat is dripping down my face, soaking my clothes. I lie down on the floor, thinking of the drop below me.

There's a battered flier beneath the luggage rack. I pull it toward me. It says:

EGLIFF* OR TRUTH??

PEOPLE...MERE PUPPETS OF TIME??

"Wait for me that I come...if I come and you are not there, I will find you...I come at any hour..." —EDT 6:5-8

ANSWERS HAD—QUESTIONS TO BE ASKED ...AS NEVER BEFORE!

*"...when I speak the names of God I leave my own spell behind
and grow in MIGHT as I become
impersonal, speaking the way of things..."*
—OAHSPE 1 1 4:82

THE NOTHING ALL THIS COMES FROM IS NONSENSE, PAIN!

DR. WERMAN will be in attendance at the **Terrestrial Inheritance Scientific Hospital** for the duration of exactly one month beginning 33 TORMAS—if you are looking for authenticated guidance, **GO!**—business hours at 6072nd Street between the Boulevard of Sealed Cisterns and the Taken Way in El Dorado. No sincere visitor turned away!

NO SINCERE VISITOR TURNED AWAY!

(*An "egliff" is the local word here for a kind of prank or joke.)

Words disappear from the page with each blink of my eyes, leaving distinct gaps. Eventually the page says:

"Egliff...when I speak...I leave...the way of things..."
Now, the paper is blank. Even the dents, creases, and stains that disfigured it are gone. The sheet is crisp and bare, like new. I can hear a cricket chirp somewhere near me. Just one cricket, and the acoustics make it sound as though it's inside a room, not outdoors. There's a low, metallic thumping too, which, though faint, is drowning out the creak and rattle of the funicular. I close my eyes to stop it.

No use. The hard, corrugated floor of the car is soft, a sheet of worn, pebbly cotton.

If I were to open my eyes, the darkness I now see would remain, even as the field of vision deepened. I know where I am.

I don't know where that is, but I know where I am. Back on earth, as always.

There's someone lying in this bed. Someone else, next to me. A stranger. I can feel the weight of another body pressing on the mattress, I hear regular, deep breathing, neutral breathing. I'm on my back, covers off, my throbbing foot is a wan streak in the dark against the bedframe. There's a mass, a long mass, a long weight, lying right next to me. Turned to the wall, on its side, all covered except for a dark head sunk deep into the pillow. Just a shape, and sound. No warmth. A neutral shape.

Something cold. Wet. And smelling. Like iron. Like iron. Spreading from that neutral shape. I am lying in it. I didn't realize, because it was so colder nor warmer than I. It's crawling, darkening the sheet, the blankets, and I smell iron. A strong odor of iron, iron. It has pooled around me.

I want with all I've got to be away from this. It's here. I want to scramble for the door, even if I have to crawl, but panic ties me to the bed, my body won't answer my brain. My ears are sharper and sharper, tuning in on that breathing, making it seem as though it were getting louder and louder and deeper and deeper when the sound isn't changing. The more intently I stare at that shape, the vaguer it gets, the harder it is to stop looking for a shape. The shape swims. The breathing is mine, only.

The body stirs. I know who it is. I feel it rolling over next to me, turning toward me.

Now it's facing me. One glance is all it would take. I would see. Seeing is the last thing in the world I want. Better a thousand years of this pain and misery than one glimpse. But opening your eyes is so easy, keeping them shut is so hard.

Maybe it will get up? Go to work?

Go to work?

I've seen before, in this house, or apartment building, or clinic, what there is to see.

It won't be sleeping.

It won't be leaving.

It will be suffering, suffering impossibly.

One day this pain is going to end. One day I'll start a dream, dream forever, and time will die before me. I tell myself that.

I think...that it's been here all the time. It's only just now that I've noticed it. Something happened in my brain. The black brane is dreaming. All of existence screams with only one voice, can have only one voice—yours.

My foot explodes.

THE END

ABOUT THE AUTHOR

Michael Cisco is an American writer, Deleuzian academic, teacher, and translator living in New York City. He is best known for his first novel, *The Divinity Student,* which won the International Horror Guild Award for Best First Novel of 1999. His novel *The Great Lover* was nominated for the 2011 Shirley Jackson Award for Best Novel of the Year, and declared the Best Weird Novel of 2011 by the Weird Fiction Review. His nonfiction book, *Weird Fiction: A Genre Study,* was nominated for a HWA Stoker award in 2023. *Pest*, a novel, was published by CLASH in 2023. He teaches at CUNY Hostos.

ALSO BY CLASH BOOKS

PEST

Michael Cisco

THE PAIN EATER

Kyle Muntz

BELOW THE GRAND HOTEL

Cat Scully

STRANGE STONES

Edward Lee & Mary SanGiovanni

8114

Joshua Hull

THE MAN WHO SAW SECONDS

Alexander Boldizar

I Can Fix Her

Rae Wilde

INVAGINIES

Joe Koch

I DIED TOO, BUT THEY HAVEN'T BURIED ME YET

Ross Jeffery

CHARCOAL

Garrett Cook